Kassie longs to yield herself to Loren's love...but she's already committed herself to God's love...

Kassie's heart was pounding in her temples. She began to push away. "Please, Loren, not so fast." For so long she had questioned and wondered, not knowing. But now... "We need to slow down. Take our time." She sought her breath and forced it back to its regular rhythm.

"Time? What does time matter? Let's not waste any more precious time."

"But Loren..." Her mind was a wild war of confusion.

"I know you feel the same about me. I can feel it when you're near me."

"Yes..." She heard the hesitation in her own voice.

"Then what is it?"

"The Lord..." she began, but he wouldn't let her finish.

He stepped back. "Don't, Kassie. Please don't."

"But it's so important to me."

"God has no part in this. No part. This is you and I. Here and now. In the reality of life. I'm telling you that I care deeply about you, and you want to toss God in the center and make it a triangle." Loren leaned his weight against a nearby tree trunk. "I can't compete against God for your love."

NORMA JEAN LUTZ began her professional writing career in 1977 when she enrolled in a writing corre- spondence course. Since then, she has had over 200 short stories and articles published in both secular and Christian publications. She is also the author of five published teen novels.

Books by Norma Jean Lutz

The Winning
Heart

Norma Jean Lutz

Heartsong Presents

To Ivar Ted Mattson:
I treasure your friendship!

A note from the Author:
I love to hear from my readers! You may write to me at the
following address:

Norma Jean Lutz
Author Relations
P.O. Box 719
Uhrichsville, OH 44683

ISBN 1-55748-679-4

THE WINNING HEART

one

A silver Mercedes rolled quietly to a stop in front of Blackburn Stables. Kassie Carver peered out from the back seat window, wondering where her sister Glorene had dragged her this time. When she had dressed that morning in a comfortable flowered jump suit, she'd had no idea she'd once again be transported into Glorene's world of commercial real estate.

"Let's go see if Harlis Blackburn is in a selling mood," Kassie's red-haired sister said to the man beside her.

"It'll be a miracle if he is," the man answered.

"A miracle? That's entirely possible." Glorene set the gear of her car in park and lifted her little poodle into her arms. Glorene's copper-colored hair was a striking contrast with the emerald suit she was wearing, and her beauty seemed to be turning the head of the pleasant, silver-haired man by her side.

Creighton Hollister had obviously grayed prematurely, for his features marked him as barely in his mid-forties. Noting the plain gold band on Creighton's left hand, Kassie was mildly disturbed at her divorced sister's open flirtation.

"Come in with us," Glorene said over her shoulder to Kassie as she stepped out of the car. "I'll need you to hold Natty while Creighton and I talk to Mr. Blackburn."

Why she had been asked to come along was a mystery to Kassie. Since the employment agency had scheduled no interviews for her, she'd planned to spend the day catching up on letters to friends back home. But that excuse hadn't been good enough for Glorene.

"Perish that thought," her sister had said in her sternest voice. "You'll stagnate sitting around this old apartment. You need to get out and meet people."

In the past six weeks since she had arrived in Westport, Virginia, Kassie felt she'd met enough people. More people, she thought, than the entire population of her home state of Wyoming.

At the front door of the stables, Glorene handed the apricot-colored poodle to Kassie. "We'll only be a few minutes," she said, then hooked her arm into Creighton's and led him toward an office door off the arena area. They were met there by a weathered old man in worn boots, faded jeans, and a plaid shirt with the sleeves rolled up. This was evidently Mr. Blackburn.

The riding club's indoor arena was deserted except for a single rider. A male rider dressed in a riding habit was repeatedly taking a chestnut-colored thoroughbred over the jumps.

Kassie smiled with pleasure as she settled on a hard bleacher seat to watch. She'd not seen a horse since leaving Cody six weeks ago. She leaned forward in excitement as she followed the fine features of the magnificent animal.

With her free hand, she tucked a stray brunette curl into the scarf-tied pony tail at the nape of her neck. Her other hand clutched the poodle.

The heady aroma of horses and leather had a nostalgic effect on her and pulled her back into memories of hours spent on horseback at her grandfather's large ranch near Jackson Hole. On the back of an agile cutting horse, she had worked alongside the men as calves were branded, earmarked, gelded, and vaccinated each year.

Her Grandpa Carver's quarter horses were never as sleek as this mount, but they were nonetheless well-trained under the old man's watchful eye. What a flagrant waste of time Grandpa Carver would have thought a riding club. Kassie could imagine him laughing out loud at the very sight of the young man in the spiffy habit. And the flat saddle? He would have scoffed: "A feller cain't even hang onto that puny thing when he's a-comin' up out of a ravine with a bawlin' calf slung across the saddle."

Kassie's eyes crinkled in a smile at the memories. She and her grandfather had been very close, and she missed him terribly. She enjoyed the memories of her years at the Double-C Ranch, but looking back, at the expense of looking courageously forward, could be dangerous.

She was here now, in Westport, hundreds of miles from the small house in Cody where she and a nurse had tenderly cared for Cal Carver until he died. In the old man's final days, he'd talked of nothing but his finest livestock *and* the anticipation of going to be with his loved ones in heaven.

"Promise me, Kassie," he'd said in one of his more pensive moods, "after I'm gone, you'll go to Virginia and get to know your sister. She's all the kin you got left, and I don't want you staying on out here alone."

"But, Grandpa," she'd protested, "I love Wyoming. What would I do in Westport?"

"Kin is kin," he had insisted. "The two of you need one another."

Kassie had seen no way she needed her ten-year-older sister who obviously hated Wyoming as passionately as Kassie loved it. Glorene ran away to marry at age seventeen, and had seldom been heard from since.

Following their grandfather's funeral in Cody two months ago, a dry-eyed Glorene moved down the steps of the white frame church. In older-sister fashion, she placed an arm about Kassie's shoulders. "There's nothing here for you now, Kassie," she had said in her low voice. "As soon as we finish up the details, you're coming back to Virginia to live with me."

The invitation sounded more like an order, but since it fell in line with Grandpa's desires, Kassie agreed. Obediently, if not fully enthusiastic, she stored much of her possessions, and two weeks after her grandfather's death, she flew halfway across the country to Westport.

The poodle in her lap was squirming and wiggling, jolting her out of her reverie. Kassie had dubbed the dog, "Naughty," after having several pairs of hose ruined by tiny claws raking down her legs.

"I suppose, Natty," she whispered to the dog, "that your lovely mistress feels she's rescuing me from a life of social deprivation." Indeed, in the short time since she had arrived, Kassie had been swept into her sister's busy lifestyle of hectic days and nights of business dates and social gatherings.

Tomorrow, however, Kassie had her own plans. The employment agency had scheduled an interview for a secretarial position at the Quillian Advertising Agency. Hopefully, when she got a job, she could eventually rent her own place and come and go as she pleased, even if her apartment could never be as plush as Glorene's downtown high-rise.

"All your fancy trappings are nice, Naughty Dog," Kassie said, stroking the animal's silky ear. "But it's too much for this little cowgirl." Natty wiggled in protest to the insulting name. "Sit still," she told him. "I wonder who dog-sat you before I arrived on the scene?"

The rider in the arena had stepped up the pace of the thoroughbred, and Kassie noted with interest that the young man was perfectly relaxed in the saddle and harmoniously in tune with the liquid movements of the regal mount. His face, however, was rigid with determination, his square jaw set in intense concentration as he took each jump.

Kassie busied Natty with half a granola bar she discovered in a torn wrapper in her jump suit pocket. When she leaned down to retrieve a fallen piece of the bar, she unconsciously loosened her grasp on the frisky dog, never dreaming he would opt for freedom over food. In a flash, he was out of her grasp and scrambling away in the direction he'd seen his mistress take. But Natty chose the shortcut—across the dirt-filled arena floor, directly into the path of the high stepping gelding.

"Natty! No!" she screamed before thinking. Of course she knew the shriek of her voice would be as startling to the horse as the streaking animal in his path.

The high-bred, high-strung horse was terrified and broke back just as he was prepared for a jump, veering sharply sideways, then rearing several times. The rider threw his entire muscular frame into clinging to the back of the frightened horse and maneuvering him. The feat was accomplished with more dexterity than many bronc riders Kassie had seen in the corral of the Double-C Ranch.

With an unbelievable calm, the young man settled the horse, stroking him and speaking to him softly as the mount returned to his senses. Dismounting, he tied the reins to the railing and strode stiffly to where Kassie was scurrying to retrieve the mischievous dog, to whom she planned to apply a sound spanking. She was also anxious to apologize to the rider as quickly as possible.

She dragged Natty out from under a saddle frame, then scrambled to her feet. Looking up at the rider, she saw that he was trembling. He was taller than she had judged him to be, tall and powerfully built. He glared at her with open disdain as he flicked his riding crop repeatedly against his leg.

"Lady," he said between his teeth, "this arena is no place for unruly dogs and screaming females. That mongrel you have there could have caused a serious accident, causing injury to me or my mount—who, by the way, is worth thousands of dollars."

"I'm so sorry...," she began.

"Sorry? Sorry won't cut it," came the sharp reply. "Obviously you have no knowledge of horses or you'd never have brought that despicable animal in here in the first place. If you have no business here to keep you, I suggest you take your mutt and your screeching voice outside."

His aloof attitude stunned her. He spoke as though she were a misbehaving child, when if he only knew, she agreed wholeheartedly that Natty had indeed behaved abominably. She wondered if the man was angry because he'd had a scare, or if this was his general behavior. She longed to inform him that she not only had practical knowledge of horses, but that she loved this one on sight and wouldn't have hurt him for anything in the world, but the set of the man's square jaw let her know he was too angry to listen at the present. She turned to go.

Abruptly, Glorene's voice sounded. "Now, now. Cool down, handsome. This mongrel, as you call him, happens to be *my* dog. My sister was holding him at *my* request." Glorene strolled toward them and, taking Natty from Kassie's arms, was decorated with wet licks on the cheek. "That was a sterling performance. Are your reflexes always that keen?" she asked, eyeing his brawny build.

"I can't really say, ma'am," the rider replied, his voice laced with sarcasm. "I've never had the opportunity to test them in quite that violent a manner."

"Don't get so uptight," Glorene cooed. "Would it help if I apologized for Natty's nasty manners? He really is a good doggie."

Kassie was embarrassed at Glorene's tactics to smooth over her poor judgment at having brought the dog.

The rider's clear blue eyes narrowed. "I fail to see the humor in this. Jolly Roger is my father's favorite mount, and he's worth a great deal of money. It would have been disastrous had he been seriously hurt."

Creighton, who had kept silent until now, stepped forward. "Excuse me. I'm Creighton Hollister, and you, I believe, are the son of attorney Vaughn Marcellus. Right?" The older man extended his hand, causing the rider to hesitate, then move the riding crop to his left hand to return the handshake.

"I recognize you, Mr. Hollister, from the TV newscasts regarding the mayor's race. I'm Loren Marcellus, and I'm pleased to meet you." He pulled off his black riding helmet and tucked it under his arm. His light brown hair was sweat-curled.

"I realize this was a most unfortunate incident," Hollister said. "However, since it was injury-free, let's drop the matter and be civil. By your command performance in the saddle, Marcellus, you look like a take-control type of guy. Mr. Blackburn, the owner here, tells me that since he closed the riding club, you're the only one allowed to ride—due to your father's influence, I presume?"

Loren's face reflected his annoyance. "Harlis Blackburn and I are close friends, and I need no influence from Attorney Marcellus for this small favor."

"I see," Creighton said slowly. "Is your father active in Mayor Bosworth's campaign?"

"If you call being campaign manager active. But you should know better than I do about such matters. I seldom see Dad since I moved out to an apartment near the university."

"Left the mansion, eh?" Creighton slipped his hand in his suit coat pocket and rocked forward on his toes as he spoke. "And attending law school, I understand. And what part are you playing in this heated campaign?"

The young rider paused. The square jaws relaxed, and Kassie could see there were deep dimples in the tanned cheeks. "My studies keep me too occupied to bother with political matters." He chose the words carefully.

"An enterprising young law student not interested in political campaigns? Especially one in which he could learn tricks of the trade first hand? Incredible." Creighton gave a slight smile.

"If you'll excuse me, Jolly Roger needs attention," Loren said, ignoring Creighton's last remark. "I have an appointment in an hour." He glanced at his watch and then at Kassie. "I apologize for lashing out at you half-cocked," he told her. "A horse shouldn't be that important to a person—but to me, he is." He spoke the comment as though it explained everything.

"I accept your apology," she said softly. Something about his clear blue eyes fascinated Kassie. They sparkled with a transparent quality which seemed to belie his stern exterior. She thought she detected a flicker of a smile before he turned to go.

"Loren," Creighton called after him, "what's your phone number? I'd like to talk business with you in the future."

Without looking back, Loren Marcellus called out the numbers and continued walking briskly toward his all-important thoroughbred.

Pensively, Kassie watched him for a moment, unaware that Glorene and her client were walking away.

"Come on, Baby," Glorene called over her shoulder, "quit ogling."

Kassie turned and obediently followed.

As Glorene nosed the Mercedes down the dusty drive from the stables, Creighton said to her, "I don't know how you did it. Harlis Blackburn has refused for months to talk to me about selling his business. How'd you get him to change his mind?"

Glorene's red curls—which Kassie knew were not their natural color—tossed lightly as she craned to watch for oncoming traffic before pulling out onto the street. "You want me to tell my trade secrets?" She gave a little ripple of laughter. "Then what would you need me for?"

"All joking aside, Glorene, you've proven yourself to me. I'm asking you to join my band wagon as my campaign manager. What do you say to that, Ms. Paquette? Is it a deal?" From her back seat vantage point, Kassie could see the intense expression on Creighton's face. "You're an excellent businesswoman and I need that to get my campaign off the ground. Otherwise, Mayor Bosworth will continue to run the city of Westport with his iron will, backed by the vicious Attorney Marcellus."

Glorene gave another little laugh. "But I know so little about politics," she protested.

"I'll teach you. It's not much different than running a

business—just more work for less pay. You know the city, and you know the people. Will you do it?"

"Let's just say I'll give it a try. But if we see it's not working out, I retain the privilege to jump ship whenever I please."

"Agreed."

Reports of Glorene's success in the field of commercial real estate had filtered back to Kassie and Grandpa in Cody, but Kassie had had little comprehension of the extent of that success until she reached the city. During the ride from the airport to downtown Westport, she was abruptly awakened to the truth by the sight of several billboards sporting her sister's picture. "Glorene Paquette Realty," announced the signs with a flourish. "Your listing for results!"

Now, Kassie felt somewhat smothered by the business and political talk and wished she were walking along the tree-lined Williamette Boulevard where they were driving. Early March sunshine was wooing the budding shade trees to prepare for their upcoming performance, and the street was graced on either side by Victorian homes with wide front porches and porch swings.

A sign in the front yard of one stately house caught her eye: "Second Floor Apartment For Rent."

How wonderful it would be to have a place of her own on just such a shady street. She determined that after today, she would refuse to allow her persuasive sister to drag her along on business ventures. Then Kassie could become more diligent in job hunting.

Remembering the embarrassment of the incident with Loren Marcellus, she wished she'd made that decision earlier. She could imagine Grandpa Carver's reaction if anyone had spooked a horse of his. Before the old man became a Christian, he made no apologies for his geyser-style temper. But Loren Marcellus had even apologized for his anger.

As Kassie thought of Loren, Creighton began talking about him. "You got me the Blackburn Stables, Glorene—now can you get me Loren Marcellus too? That fellow is brimming over with potential."

Glorene steered her car into the cool recesses of the underground garage beneath the apartment building where she lived. Turning off the ignition, she looked at Creighton. "For the future mayor of Westport, Virginia? Anything! Would you like him on a silver platter—or on the thoroughbred?" Glorene released her lilting laughter and patted Hollister's arm.

"Seriously, Glorene. He could be a strategic tool in our campaign."

"You think so? Well then, I'll do my best. Boss."

Once again, Kassie was irritated by her sister's undisguised flirting with the gentle Mr. Hollister. Purposely, she released the struggling Natty, who bounded into the front seat and into the arms of his mistress.

"Here's the real pro," Glorene said, hugging the silky squirming bundle. "Natty put Loren to the test for sure."

Riding the elevator up to the apartment, Kassie realized afresh how foreign this life was to her. Surely her grandfather hadn't meant for two sisters—who were worlds apart—to become *this* close.

two

The breakfast alcove adjacent to the kitchen was Kassie's favorite room in Glorene's spacious apartment. Lemon yellow curtains and daisy-print wallpaper came alive to meet the morning sun streaming in the tall windows. Nearby, French doors led out to the terrace balcony. The air was still too cool to eat breakfast on the terrace, the housekeeper Leomia informed her, but Kassie would have liked to try.

From the terrace was a stunning view of the shimmering ocean, a source of fascination to Kassie, having come from landlocked Wyoming. When Glorene was gone, Kassie enjoyed standing out on the sweeping terrace talking to the Lord and breathing deeply of the salty breezes that came in off the azure waters.

As she stepped into the alcove for breakfast, dressed for her interview, the stoutly-built Leomia gave a low whistle. "You look right sharp there, Kassie."

"Thanks, Leomia. Sharp enough for an important interview?" She'd been in a stew about what to wear. Her wardrobe was limited, but she'd finally chosen a tailored suit with a ruffled blouse. She wasn't sure, though, if it was right for the atmosphere of an advertising agency.

"Take my word for it. You look great." Leomia emphasized the comment with a pat on Kassie's back as she poured coffee and set out steaming biscuits.

The two had had an affinity for one another since their

first encounter. The no-nonsense, gray-haired Leomia had mannerisms much like Grandpa Carver, and the new friendship helped to ease Kassie's loneliness.

Glorene, though, seemed totally oblivious to her younger sister's grief over their grandfather's death. And since Glorene had no love for Wyoming, she was also oblivious to Kassie's homesickness.

"Are you nervous about the interview?" Leomia asked.

"A little, I suppose."

"Didn't you tell me you graduated from a business school? And learned to use all them fancy computers?"

Kassie nodded as she buttered a biscuit. "I have the training, but because of Grandpa's illness, I only worked through temporary agencies. My job experience is a bit thin."

"Aw, don't you worry none, honey." Leomia looked at her with gentle brown eyes and a wide smile. "It's the Lord who opens the doors in your life, and He closes them. Can't nobody stand in your way when God is opening the right doors."

Kassie returned the smile. "Of course you're right. Thanks for reminding me."

Their mutual love of the Lord had drawn Kassie and Leomia together quickly. The day Kassie arrived, Leomia noticed the Bible among Kassie's things, and her brown cheeks glowed with pleasure. "It's about time someone invited the Lord in this place besides me," she quipped.

Glorene saw the Bible too, but her reaction was quite different. "There's no place for your religion here, Baby," she told Kassie with a toss of her copper curls. "You'll find that out soon enough. This is a dog-eat-dog world you've come to. Nothing like Grandpa's quiet place in

Jackson Hole."

Now, as Kassie and Leomia were talking, Glorene strolled into the alcove, clad in a trailing olive-colored robe and yawning widely in mock protest at having been awakened. "Well, I'll tell you two chattering magpies something about opening doors," she said grandly. "Glorene Paquette opens all the doors in *her* life. And nobody had better stand in the way when I decide to come on through." She seated her willowy frame across the table from Kassie.

Leomia pressed her lips together for a moment as she set a delicate blue cup and saucer in front of her employer. "Maybe so, Miss Glorene," she said thoughtfully. "Maybe so. But if you'd let the Lord do the opening, they'd be all the *right* doors."

Kassie watched her sister's face and frowned. Glorene obviously assumed she was humoring the elderly lady by allowing her to speak her piece, never realizing that Leomia's concern was deep and heartfelt.

"I'd better step it up, or I'll be late." Kassie drained the last of her coffee. "Leomia, which bus do I catch to find this place?" Kassie showed her a slip of paper containing the address, knowing Leomia was a veteran of the Westport bus lines.

Glorene spoke up. "The bus? You can't expect to find a job if you have to stand around at the bus stops all day. Just hang on to your hat a sec, Baby, and I'll drive you."

The nickname of "Baby" was tolerated by Kassie only because she assumed that owing to their years apart, Glorene had yet to realize she'd grown into an adult. But now the thought of being chauffeured to a job interview in a Mercedes, as though she were a child being taken to piano lessons, was stifling.

"Glorene," Kassie said, holding her voice steady, "if you take me in your car, they won't even think I *need* a job. And if they give me those long aptitude tests, you'll have to wait around for hours." She knew Glorene detested waiting—for anyone.

"Well," her sister demurred, "I suppose you're right. But at least wait until I can get you cab money. The bus is such a drag."

Kassie wanted to resist further, but Glorene was already headed down the hall to her bedroom.

Leomia gave her an understanding pat on the arm. "Don't you fret. Your sis hasn't had a chance to help anyone for a long time," she whispered. "It's kinda good for her to be looking out for someone other than the old number one all the time."

Kassie gave Leomia a gentle hug of thanks before leaving the apartment, with cab money in hand. The woman's tenderness was heartwarming.

As the cab sped out to the suburbs, she observed that Quillian's was located near the Blackburn Stables. Briefly, she thought of the previous day and let her mind picture the expert horsemanship of Loren Marcellus. She wondered about this man who was evidently an enterprising law student, the son of an influential attorney, and also an avid horse lover. Interesting combination. But she was certain of one thing—he was much too aloof and hotheaded for her taste. More to her liking was his horse, Jolly Roger.

Often as a child she had dreamed of riding with the precision and skill Loren displayed. The day the Double-C Ranch was sold, along with all the horses and her own beloved Onrushing Charger, had been devastating for her. Her grandfather, however, was simply too old and too ill to operate the ranch any longer.

Ted Winters, the widower who purchased the ranch, encouraged her to return and ride any time she liked, but she never felt the same. If Ted had had his way, though, she could have become Mrs. Ted Winters and retained the ranch forever.

"I know you're mighty fond of young Winters," Grandpa Carver counseled her, "but don't let your love for the ranch suck you into a marriage not built on genuine love."

He needn't have worried. The rangy cowboy was kind, and sincere in his offer, but to marry without love was not an option for Kassie. She doted on Ted's children, little Jessica with the mop of curls and the toddler Joseph, and often Ted reminded her how they needed a mother—but even her love of his children could not lure her into marriage.

The cab pulled to a stop in front of a new office building, landscaped about the entrance with skinny young trees and freshly unrolled sod, prematurely green. Kassie paid the driver with the money Glorene had given her, and hurried into the building. Quillian's Advertising Agency was located on the top floor.

The personnel manager, a soft-spoken fortyish man, was cordial. The interview went smoothly, and she felt confident of her high test scores. After several hours, when she assumed she was to be dismissed, he surprised her by saying she was now to meet Ed Quillian. He ushered her into a paneled office where a balding, heavy-set man sat behind a massive mahogany desk. The man stood as she entered and greeted her with a handshake across the desk, stretching his short arm to reach her.

"Ms. Carver, I'm Ed Quillian, President of Quillian Advertising Agency. Please sit down."

Kassie could see her application and test forms lying in front of him where he had obviously been reviewing them. "Thank you, sir," she answered as she puzzled over being called into his office. "I'm pleased to meet you." Could she already be under serious consideration for this position?

"Ms. Carver, as you can see, we're a first class agency— and your test scores show that you're a very capable young lady. Mr. Bates, our personnel manager, was instructed to bring to my attention any applicant who had very high test scores and who was also quite attractive. It's vital that we maintain our image, you see." He peered at her over a pair of small reading glasses.

Kassie reddened uncomfortably. Unsure how to reply, she simply said, "I'm glad to hear you're pleased with the test results." Wasn't it against some discrimination law to take appearance into consideration? What if Mr. Bates had thought her ugly?

The portly Mr. Quillian was still studying her. "Would you be able to begin work the first of next week?"

The abruptness of the question surprised her. She'd been so anxious for a job, so ready to earn her own way, but now she felt unsettled by the pressure to make a quick decision.

Noting her hesitancy, Mr. Quillian went on, "I've had other applicants, Ms. Carver, whose work experience excels yours. I'm sure you're aware that experience counts for a great deal."

"I am aware of that. But I was unable to work after

graduation because of caring for my grandfather." She felt herself stalling. But why? Something wasn't quite right inside her.

"Is it the money? I assure you, the salary you receive here won't be matched in many other offices in Westport." He placed the impressive figures before her. "We're a successful agency. Best in this area," he persisted. "You can be proud to be a member of our organization. What's your decision?"

With that kind of salary, she could easily move out of Glorene's apartment and find her own place. Pushing her uneasiness aside, she agreed. "I see no reason why I can't begin next Monday morning. Thank you, sir, for the offer."

Ed Quillian's round face lit up, and he stood to his feet. "Good! That's excellent. You have good taste, my dear. Now let me introduce you to your new boss." His stubby finger pushed the button on the phone as he asked for Sean to be sent in.

Presently, at the door stood a fair-skinned, slender man dressed in a business suit; he looked at Kassie with mischievous, laughing eyes. "You called me, sir?" he asked without taking his eyes from Kassie's face.

"Ms. Carver, this is my nephew, Sean Quillian Phipps. Sean, meet your newly-hired secretary, Ms. Kassie Carver." Having said that, Mr. Quillian seated himself and sighed heavily, as though he had completed a monumental task.

"Kassie—a lovely name for a lovely girl." Sean stepped over to her chair. As he reached for her hand, she felt the blood rush to her cheeks.

"Hello," she said rather stiffly, reluctantly offering her

hand. He held it for a moment in something unlike a handshake. Gently, she pulled her hand back.

"Ms. Carver's agreed to begin work next Monday, Sean," Mr. Quillian informed him.

"Not tomorrow?" Sean asked, causing his uncle to give a dry laugh. Sean's pale green eyes were accented by sandy brows and lashes. His reddish-blond hair was neatly styled, giving him a professional appearance, despite his youthful features.

"Do you want to see her test scores?" Mr. Quillian asked, holding up a sheaf of papers.

Sean shook his head, grinning. "She's already scored, sir."

At that moment, had there been any way to back out of the job, Kassie would have cashed it all in and hurried home. But she'd never been a quitter. She had agreed, and now she would follow through. Just like Cal Carver had taught her.

"I'll try my level best to be a good secretary, Mr. Phipps," she said. "I've had excellent training." Deliberately, she rose to leave, anxious to make her departure and clear her mind.

"Please, I'm Sean to you," he said with a wide smile. "And I have no reason to doubt your capabilities in running an efficient office."

Kassie hurriedly said her good-byes and was thankful to be outside again. With quick steps, she headed down the sidewalk in search of a nearby bus stop.

Out in the spring air, Sean and his uncle didn't seem quite so threatening. Possibly Sean was harmless, just a little frisky, like a new calf in springtime. If he were anything more, Kassie felt sure she could handle him. The offices would be a comfortable place in which to work. The pert receptionist was friendly, as were the other people she'd met. She was plenty ready to make new friends on her own.

Although this side of town had no view of the ocean or the bustling port, it was much more lovely than downtown. Kassie felt sure she could be happy working out here. Later, when Mr. Hollister re-opened the Blackburn Stables, perhaps she could ride some evenings after work. The thought of being back astride a horse bolstered her spirits even more.

Kassie approached the bus stop and waited only a short time before boarding one marked "downtown." The bus had lumbered along for a few blocks when she saw it again—the big homey-looking house with the rent sign out front. She was too late to stop and look at it now, but soon she'd return and check it out.

In the distance, the Westport skyline loomed gray-blue against the sky. With a job of her own and an apartment of her own, this city could perhaps become bearable for her.

three

The chance to check out the apartment came two days later when Glorene was away for the afternoon. Kassie boarded the bus and then watched carefully for the stately old house, anxious she might miss it. The bus' air brakes squealed as she signaled her stop, and she quickly disembarked.

She studied the delicate lattice work on the wide front porch. Climbing roses draped the lattice with a heavy network, giving promise of fragrant blossoms when the weather warmed.

In answer to her knock, the front door was opened by an elderly lady whose twinkling blue eyes studied Kassie. The face was etched with wrinkles and laugh lines, and her shoulders were a bit stooped.

"I've come to look at the apartment for rent," Kassie explained.

"Of course, my dear," the woman answered, gently ushering Kassie inside. "I'm Mrs. Myrtle Tinsley, but the girls here call me Mom Tinsley. You can too, if you like."

In her soft, southern voice, Mom Tinsley explained that she rented only to women. "When men friends visit, please see to it they come only to the parlor."

A genteel southern lady, Kassie thought as she followed her up the stairs past the dark landing. Muted light glowed from two small stained glass windows at the turn of the stairs.

The available apartment was to the right at the end of the hall. Tall open windows graced a spacious living room. The kitchen was compact and efficient. The price was reasonable, and the atmosphere was inviting. But although Kassie desperately wanted to move in immediately, she knew she would be unwise to speak for it now.

"Thanks you for taking the time to show the apartment," she said as she clasped the older lady's veined hand in her own. "But it'll be some time before I know for sure if I can take it."

On the bus returning into downtown, she wondered if she had been wise to even take the time to look. Now she wanted to move out more than ever.

❧

On Friday evening, Kassie joined Leomia on the brocade couch in the front room to watch the evening news as Creighton Hollister formally announced his intention to run for mayor of Westport, naming Glorene Paquette as his campaign manager. The appointment, they heard, was causing no small stir among Hollister's close cronies in the party ranks.

"Due only to the fact," Leomia said in her most sagacious manner, "that they don't know about your sister's cool business head. In my humble opinion, Mr. Hollister couldn't have made a wiser choice. And I think he'll make Westport a great mayor."

Leomia's love and loyalty to Glorene was a marvel to Kassie. Especially after witnessing the cold treatment the housekeeper often received from her employer, Kassie wondered that Leomia didn't just give up and quit.

The meeting at Glorene's apartment on Saturday evening was no doubt Hollister's diplomatic way of drawing his political team together. The heavy sounds of voices filtered into the kitchen where Kassie prepared a cup of hot tea, grabbed a half-empty box of crackers, and then retreated to her room before any of Glorene's guests happened in on her.

For once her sister had not insisted upon her presence at the party in progress—for which Kassie was more than grateful. Nor had Glorene requested Leomia to come in on her day off to help with the impromptu gathering. So Kassie had helped that afternoon with a few of the preparations.

"The guests who are coming tonight are the pillars of the political structure in Westport—good friends and sort of good friends of Creighton's," Glorene explained as they were arranging shrimp canapes on the cranberry-glass platters. "Of course you could join us if you want, but it'll probably be a bore. Mostly political talk."

This was the first time since she had arrived that her sister had given her a choice in the matter. Not that Glorene was intentionally being unkind. She was, quite simply, a strong-willed person accustomed to giving orders. After all, how else could she have built such a strong real estate firm?

Back in her own room, Kassie kicked off her slippers, pushed the door shut with her bare foot, and set the snack on the desk. She was grateful to be in the quiet room rather than in the midst of the noisy living room, where she'd already spent too many endless evenings.

Scattered across her desk were several papers on which she'd calculated income she knew she could count on in the near future, including the salary from her new job.

When Grandpa Carver sold the ranch, the greater part of the profits had been spent paying off past debts. In the ensuing years, much of the remainder was spent for medication and doctors, plus a part-time nurse and rent for the small house in Cheyenne where they had lived in spartan style. Cal Carver gave his young granddaughter full control of the finances, and she had managed efficiently.

The money that remained following the old rancher's death was to be divided between the two sisters, which had astonished Glorene. "I can't take that money," she told Kassie as they sat together in the little house following the funeral. "You keep it all. You took care of him all these years. I don't need it." She shook her head, and gave a rueful laugh. "I have more money now than I can keep track of."

But Kassie refused. "Grandpa wanted to be fair," she said. "The money wasn't willed to you on the basis of your possessions, but on the basis of his love. Give to charity in his name if you like, but please accept it."

Glorene's green eyes were reflective a moment. "I suppose the old man did love me some, but after Mother and Daddy died, and he and Grandma took us, I thought he hated me. He was always yelling at me. After Grandma died, it was worse. I had to get out. You don't remember those days, Kassie."

"I remember more than you think I do, but he *did* change," Kassie replied, trying to make the most of a tender moment. "After he asked Jesus into his heart, he did change. I wish you could have known him after his heart was softened."

"Ridiculous!" Glorene gave a scoffing laugh. "It was a clear cut case of his liking you better than me. And who could blame him? You're such a little sweetie." With that Glorene ended the conversation by giving her little sister a rare hug.

And now, studying the figures spread before her on the

desk, Kassie was trying to decide how she could afford that little apartment. She would be presumptuous to count on salary from her new job, but she needed to plan ahead.

Sipping the hot tea, she dug her toes into the plush carpet, and tried to imagine what having a place all her own would be like. She leaned back in the chair and looked about her at the elaborate wall hangings and the custom draperies, puzzled by the unexplainable trapped feelings that were dragging her down. Glorene was more than willing to allow her to live here indefinitely, and Kassie had no real reason not to enjoy it, yet she had experienced more freedom when caring for her invalid grandfather than she did now living in Glorene's home.

Another nagging thought persisted: the mixed feelings she had about her job at Quillian's. She looked once again at the figures on the paper before her which represented her upcoming salary. Should she make a decision based on a job with which she wasn't entirely comfortable?

She laid down her pen. That settled it! For now she would not even consider renting her own place. No matter how she felt about Glorene's lifestyle, not even Kassie missed her chance at the cozy little apartment at Mom Tinsley's. After all, the city would have other rentals, she told herself. She mustn't let emotions rule.

She rose from the desk and carried her teacup to the velvet chaise beside the bed. Settling down on the soft cushions, she picked up her worn Bible, turned to her marked place, and read from Hebrews, "...let us lay aside every weight and the sin which doth so easily beset us and let us run with patience the race that is set before us."

"Running with patience." She smiled to herself at God's sense of humor. "I've always thought of Glorene as being the impatient one, but now that I've seen that apartment,

I'm the one who is being impatient. Forgive me, Lord, and give me a heart to win the race using *Your* rules." Gently she stroked the marked page. "If that apartment is to be mine, I'll trust You to hold my reservations."

A faint rapping at her door startled her from her prayers. "Kassie! You in bed yet?"

"No, Glorene. Come in."

"All the guests have left but two, and we're going out to eat." Her sister crossed the room with an imploring look in her green eyes. The delicate features in her face reflected a deep weariness. "Please come with us, Sis. We'd love to have you."

Kassie had planned to get up early the next morning and attend a nearby church she'd located. She was anxious to get settled into a local congregation. That excuse, however, would never have convinced her sister that she needed to stay home and get her rest.

"You said it earlier, Glorene, political talk is above my head," Kassie began her polite refusal. "I'd be dead weight. You go on and have a good time."

"Honestly, Baby," Glorene persisted, "the shop talk is over and we're going to unwind. You need to get out, you know. Change into something bright and pretty and come on."

The invitation, as usual, had transformed into a firm request. Suddenly Mom Tinsley's house on the shady boulevard appealed to Kassie more than ever.

Glorene had conveniently failed to say that the two remaining guests were men—Creighton Hollister and Loren Marcellus. Kassie masked her irritation. Had she been told the truth, she would have insisted on staying home. But presently she was being escorted by Loren into a dimly lit dinner club called the Rhapsody.

The air was veiled with gray smoke and muffled conversations. The pianist in the corner was coaxing melancholy tunes from the keys. At Creighton's request, they were seated at a table concealed by lattice partitions and large potted palms.

"The press will be dogging my heels from this point on," he was saying to Glorene and Loren. "I'll count on the two of you to block and tackle for me."

Kassie assumed this meant Loren had agreed to join sides with Hollister, even though his father was campaign manager for the incumbent Mayor Bosworth. The political scene was an enigma that Kassie couldn't unravel, nor was she sure she wanted to. It was all so cloak-and-dagger.

The promise of no shop talk was quickly forgotten by Glorene, who seemed to have no inclination to speak of anything else. As the conversation floated about Kassie, as thick as the cigarette smoke, she felt like an interloper. She glanced at Loren, but his attention was captured by rapid-fire bits of information shot at him by Glorene and Creighton.

"What'll it be?" asked a somber waiter. "Something to drink?"

After the others had placed their orders, Kassie asked for a glass of iced tea.

Loren studied her with interest. "You don't drink?" he asked.

She shook her head. "No."

"Come now, Baby," her sister said in sing-song fashion. "You can let your hair down with us. We're all friends here. Just order a little screwdriver. Surely your big old God won't mind a little orange juice. It's healthy even!"

The sharp remark caught Kassie off guard. She tried to

think of an answer without making things worse.

"Ms. Paquette," Loren broke in, his blue eyes mildly humorous as he looked at Glorene, "weren't we speaking earlier this evening of people who were independent and free thinkers? Is it possible those qualities are being demonstrated here and we're not recognizing it as such?" Glancing up at the waiter, he said, "Cancel the Scotch. Make that *two* iced teas."

Kassie felt she was being patronized by the intensely handsome Marcellus, much as he might join in a game of make-believe to humor a child. However, she was still grateful that Glorene had been quieted.

Talk had turned to the subject of the Blackburn Stables, and Kassie learned that Loren had been drawn in as a consultant. He aired many lucrative suggestions for the club's improvements before reopening.

"Perhaps," Glorene said, "Kassie here could be of some help. She was practically raised in the saddle on our grandfather's ranch in Wyoming. She'd know the ins and outs of the office too because of her secretarial training. Right, Baby?" The curtness of a few moments ago had disappeared.

"In the saddle?" Once again, Loren's clear eyes were studying her from across the table. "Why didn't you tell me that the other day?"

"Forget the other day." Glorene waved her scarlet nails in the air. "That's ancient history."

"Glorene," Kassie said, finding a moment to speak for herself, "you've been so busy, I haven't had the opportunity to tell you. I begin next Monday as a secretary at Quillian's Advertising Agency."

"Quillian's?" Glorene raised her eyebrows in surprise. "Without references from me or anything? Well, what do you know about that? My little sister. That agency's done work for me in the past. They're tops in Westport." Glorene sipped her drink thoughtfully. "Isn't Ed's nephew on staff there now?"

"Sean Quillian Phipps," Kassie put in. "I'll be his secretary."

"New young blood," Glorene said to Creighton with a smile. "Could be an opportunity to get another one in our camp. And a little gratis wouldn't be anything to sneeze at. Especially with our budget."

Creighton threw back his head and laughed heartily. "Glorene, I swear. Your mind is a steel trap. Always set to spring."

Kassie shifted in her chair, wishing she'd never come. Surely Glorene wouldn't ask her to influence her new employer. The matter was too incredulous to even consider. Kassie could see more and more clearly that a time was coming when she would have to stand up to her older sister. Whether she could accomplish that with the two of them remaining on good terms was yet to be seen.

Abruptly, the quiet of their corner was disrupted when a bear of a man in a wheel chair pushed his way through the potted palms right up to their table. "Thought I heard a familiar laugh," he said in a tart, husky voice. "Share the joke, Hollister?"

"Dad!" Loren's voice registered surprise, but his blue eyes remained cool and steady.

Creighton leaned back in his chair and smiled stiffly. "Hello, Vaughn. What's a nice guy like you doing in a place like this?"

"Looking to see what's lurking in the corners, away from watchful eyes," the crusty intruder shot back.

"Dad, this is..." Loren started.

"And I'm not addressing you!" Attorney Marcellus muttered through tight lips.

Kassie could see Loren's square jaw in the older man's face, but there the resemblance ended. Loren's eyes were quiet—troubled, but quiet. His father's eyes smoldered with fiery anger.

"Now, now, Vaughn," Glorene was cooing. "No need to get in a snit. We're just having a little get-together. Wanted Loren to meet my little sister who recently moved here from Wyoming."

Dragged in once again, Kassie thought. But the comment was lost on the man bound to the wheelchair. He was interested in other matters.

"Tell me, Hollister, how is Alexandria?" Vaughn asked pointedly.

The suave Creighton, whom Kassie had never seen taken off guard, seemed momentarily unable to answer.

"Your wife, Hollister. Remember?" Vaughn twisted the verbal knife further. "How is she?"

"Fine," Creighton answered at last. "She's fine now. Should be good as new very soon. Thank you, Marcellus. And how is Victoria?"

"Victoria," came the emphatic answer, "is at *home* where she belongs. Shall I report to Mayor Bosworth that the opposing forces are gathering momentum and personnel?" His steely gaze traveled over each of them slowly, mechanically.

"Report anything you like," Creighton retorted coolly. "Just make sure the reports are factual."

"Factual?" The older Marcellus gave a hollow laugh. "Factual? Hollister, you're a rich one. Wait'll I tell that one to Bosworth." With that, he spun the metal chair around with arms as muscular as his son's.

"My father knows nothing of the rules of fair play," Loren warned when Vaughn was out of hearing.

"What do you think he'll do, now that he knows you're with us?" Creighton asked.

Loren shook his head. "I don't know. My advice is that you understand his capabilities and be ready for anything."

"That I can do." Creighton drained the last of his drink.

Kassie was wearied with this unstructured evening and silently calculated excuses for leaving.

Just then, Loren stood to his feet. "If you have no further business with me, sir," he spoke to Hollister, "I'll go on home. I'll be working out with Jolly Roger all day tomorrow, getting him ready for the big show."

"Of course," Creighton answered. "I'll give you a call Monday with further instructions. Glorene and I have a few loose ends to tie up here, but you go on."

Perceptively, Loren looked at Kassie. "How about a lift? This chit-chat must be a thorough bore to you."

"Oh yes!" Glorene piped up before Kassie could answer. "Would you, Loren? Here," she fished about in her purse and thrust a few bills at him. "I'll pay for the cab if you'll take her back to my place. That's a dear."

Loren pushed the money back across the table. "You needn't pay the way, Ms. Paquette. I'd *like* to take Kassie home."

"Oh." Glorene's expression was blank, as though she could not comprehend that Loren would want to keep company with her prudish little sister.

Kassie on the other hand was much too tired to even consider that he had, in effect, offered to take her home. Not until they were alone in the cab, the city lights reflecting on Loren's tanned face, did she begin to wonder what he was really like and why he'd even bothered.

four

"It seems to me," Loren said as the cab sped through the sparse late-night traffic, "that apologies are in order."

"Apologies?" She looked up at him. "Whatever for?"

"My thoughtless and childish outburst at the arena for starters. It occurred to me that since you've met my father, you might think I'm angry by nature. You know, the old 'like father, like son.' Actually, angry outbursts aren't my usual style. I'm sorry you were the brunt of it."

That he wanted to apologize again was touching, but he needn't have mentioned his father; obviously, they were worlds apart in nature, perhaps like her and Glorene. *Strange,* she mused, *that blood kin could be so distant and different from one another.*

"I accepted your apology the first time," she reminded him. "Anyway, it was partly my fault. You were right about the arena being no place for the dog. I could have easily taken him out. But I was entranced watching Jolly Roger take the jumps."

"You like him?"

She nodded. "He's magnificent." After a moment, she added, "You said *apologies*—as in more than one."

"For tonight." He gazed out the side window, not looking at her. "You were ill at ease at the club. I'd like to apologize for our behavior. We were thoughtless and crude asking you to endure that environment."

Kassie gave a light laugh. "You're very perceptive. And

36

I'm not a very good actress. It's kind of you to apologize, but it certainly wasn't your fault. I only wish Glorene could sense my feelings. I guess I'm a puzzle to her. She feels I've missed out on the exciting things in life and she's determined to make it up to me in one cram course." She laughed again at the thought.

"Well, have you?"

"Have I what?"

"Missed the exciting things in life?"

A nearby neon sign flooded the taxi's interior with hues of blue and green as they paused for a traffic light. In the soft flashing, Kassie turned to see a questioning expression on Loren's face. His presence seemed to fill the small space inside the taxi.

"Everyone's ideas about life are different, I suppose." She pushed dark curls back over her shoulder. "To me, it's exciting to know I have a Savior who loves me. It doesn't sound too flashy to the world, but it offers a great deal of stability in a shaky society. In Glorene's eyes, I live a hopelessly boring existence. And likewise, her lifestyle is too hectic for me."

Kassie watched for Loren to flinch as she shared God's reality, but he was still relaxed beside her, one broad hand draped over his knee, the other across the back of the seat. Still, she was certain, knowing his background, he must think her a little prissy.

"So why do you stick around?" he asked after a moment. "A girl with your intelligence could make a go of it on her own." His hand touched her shoulder as he spoke, as though to emphasize the words.

The touch sent a wave of emotion coursing through her. She kept her eyes ahead. "I'm staying with Glorene because Grandpa Carver wanted us to be together." She tried not to sound flippant or ungrateful. "I'm sure he had good reason to make the request, and I've tried to respect that. But I'd much rather be back on the open prairies of Wyoming."

"What does Wyoming have that Virginia lacks?"

"It's not that. I can't bring it down to a comparison of geography. There's an atmosphere out there, a fierce ruggedness about Wyoming's land—almost like an essence—that pulls at me deep inside."

She stopped. She'd told no one of her private feelings for several months. Her eyes were stinging with tears, but female tears seemed so manipulative. She fought them back and took a breath to continue. "When I watched you in the arena the other day, I realized how much I miss riding as well. Jolly Roger is a great performer. Even Grandpa Carver would have been impressed. And Grandpa didn't impress easily."

"Jolly Roger's a powerful horse, loaded with potential. And very important to my father," Loren explained, "which means he must be very important to me as well. As you saw the other day, that importance makes me as nervous as a wet cat."

"The horse belongs to your father?" Remembering the overbearing man in the wheelchair, Kassie wondered how much influence the man had over his own son.

"Not exactly. He belonged to my brother Roger."

"*Belonged*? Doesn't your brother want him any more?" Kassie couldn't imagine anyone giving up such a tremendous horse.

"Roger is dead." The tone was flat.

"Oh. I'm so sorry." She looked at him. He was staring

out the window, the square jaw, the straight nose, the high cheekbones silhouetted by lights outside the cab. "When?"

"About a year ago." He drew in a sigh. "Roger was a year younger than I—the perfect son for Vaughn Marcellus. Lacking only in the area of ruthlessness. You remind me of Roger when you speak of God so easily."

"Do I?" *A brother who loved God, and a father who hates everyone.* Kassie wondered where Loren stood with God, and where his life was headed. "What happened to Roger?" she asked cautiously, unsure if he wanted to talk about him.

"Dad had planned a backpacking trip to Canada, and he invited me to go along. I was fed up with his interference in my life. We argued about everything. When I refused to go, he pulled Roger out of school during finals week and took him instead. Roger always said yes, no matter what the cost. He contended that loving Dad would do more good than fighting with him." Loren's hand that had been loose over his knee curled into a tight fist. "They were flying back into camp, when the small plane went down. Roger was killed instantly and Dad's legs were paralyzed."

The cab at that moment pulled to a stop in front of Glorene's apartment building, but Loren was oblivious to the clicking meter.

"So much for what Christian love gained Roger. Made him into a martyr. And for what? A waste. The waste of a wonderful life."

Loren's tall frame had gone taut as he had spoken of the loss. The pain was as fresh for him as the loss of Grandpa was for her. And yet Grandpa had died after living a full rich life; Roger had been cut down in the vibrancy of youth. Silently, she prayed for Loren, for the gentle Spirit of the Lord to heal his wounds.

"He was doing what he thought right," she said gently. "That's an admirable quality."

"A senseless waste," he said again, as though he hadn't heard.

"It's late. I'd better go. Thanks for bringing me home."

He turned then and their eyes met. "I'm sorry, Kassie. I didn't mean to lose myself in past history."

"Don't apologize. I asked."

Quickly, Loren stepped out and stood tall on the curb, reaching down to assist her. "I'll walk you up."

"No!" she answered too hastily. Then more softly, "That's not necessary. But thank you anyway." Of course he was only being polite. But she needed to get away from him.

His hand was on her arm. "May I see you again?"

Something inside her wanted to lay her own hand over his and hold it. She pulled away with a nervous laugh. "No doubt you'll see me again. Probably without a choice." She turned to go.

Suddenly, her face was in his hands, and his warm lips were covering hers. Briefly, she submitted to the gentle strength and tenderness of his strong arms. Her heart had stopped, her breath was gone.

"Thanks for listening, Kassie," he whispered.

She couldn't answer, but pulled away and ran into the building.

Her heart was pounding as she got ready for bed. She was trembling so she could hardly pull her dress over her head. It smelled of cigarette smoke, but traces of Loren's spicy cologne lingered there as well. How strange that in the short time she'd spent with Loren she felt like a woman again, for the first time since arriving at Westport. Glorene often made her feel like a misplaced child.

But she should never have let him kiss her. Plenty of women must already be in the life of a man like Loren. One kiss, more or less, would mean nothing to him.

At the club she had felt exhausted, but now she was wide awake. She wrapped her fleece robe around her, grabbed her Bible, and curled up on the bed. She browsed through Psalms and Proverbs, looking for comfort. "Trust in the Lord with all thine heart," she read aloud softly, "and lean not unto thine own understanding. In all thy ways acknowledge Him and He shall direct thy paths." She put her head down against her bent knees. "I acknowledged You to Loren, Lord. I never want to be ashamed of You. Don't let my head be turned by such a handsome, unattainable man. I need Your wisdom."

When she awoke the next morning, she was still outside the covers and the open Bible lay beside her.

The church she chose to attend this morning was large but friendly. She was given a visitor's name tag to wear, and several people warmly welcomed her. Someone handed her a schedule of Sunday School classes, as well as an activities list for the singles group. She took the paper eagerly, for she wanted to get involved as quickly as possible. Her heart soared as she joined in the singing. Singing praises to the Lord lifted her spirits like nothing else could.

The church service bolstered her for the coming week's challenges. When Monday morning dawned brilliant and mildly warm for March, she was ready for it.

Spring arrived earlier here than in Wyoming. According to the weather report, snow flurries sweeping out of the Rockies were dumping the white stuff across her home state today. In Virginia, though, the sun was shining and spring was in the air.

As she walked to the bus stop, all the bad premonitions about working at Quillian's had melted like so much fog in the bright sunshine. Honeybees flitted about the dandelions which had made their brazen appearance around the bench where she waited for the bus.

Thankfully, Glorene had been distracted by a phone call when Kassie was leaving and was prevented from calling a cab. Kassie could never seem to find an effective way to refuse Glorene's extensions of kindness without riling her anger.

The bus driver returned her smile and greeting. Before reaching the Quillian agency, the bus topped a hill and there lay the low-slung buildings of Blackburn Stables, surrounded by expanses of greening hills. Off to the west was a vast wooded area which she knew to be laced with riding trails. It was a beautiful piece of property, and Kassie wondered if Creighton Hollister had purchased it only for the riding club, or if he planned to develop it into other investment ventures. She would hate to see angry bulldozers topple the trees to make way for a shopping mall. Although she felt that Creighton was an honest man, he was at the same time a shrewd businessman.

Other than Vaughn's sharp remarks at the club on Saturday night, no one had ever mentioned Creighton's wife in Kassie's hearing. The bits of conversation there had stirred up her curiosity.

Within minutes, however, matters of real estate and politics were forgotten as she stepped into the smartly decorated offices of Quillian's on the fifth floor. There she was shown to her office by the friendly receptionist, Wendy.

Wendy was assigned to show Kassie the office routines and explain company policies. The morning flew by as they studied the files and shuffled through the papers stacked on the desk.

Sean Phipps, Wendy informed Kassie, was out of town for a couple of days, which gave her time to acclimate herself to the new job. The phones were busy, and Kassie soon learned how Sean wanted his calls and correspondence handled.

Returning home that evening, Kassie felt certain she was going to enjoy the job. The feeling of independence was glorious. When the bus lumbered past Mom Tinsley's, she craned to see if the sign was still out front. It was. On Friday evening, she decided, with her first paycheck in hand, she'd stop and put down a deposit against the rent and set in motion her plans to move.

The next afternoon, Sean returned with several tapes full of reports and correspondence recorded while he was away. His manner of the previous week seemed to dissolve as he briefed her with precise instructions. Kassie was thankful she'd studied the files and was able to answer intelligibly as he gave directions. Only at one point did he look at her affectionately and comment, "It's great having you here, Kassie. We're going to get along famously."

Later, Sean waved toward the bar in the alcove off his office. "Take a minute," he said to her, "and fix us both a drink, would you, please?"

Her breath caught short in her throat. "I don't drink, Sean," she told him, "and I've never poured a drink in my life. I'm sure one you fixed yourself would be much better."

The smiling eyes sobered. "You're kidding. The next thing you know you'll be telling me you teach Sunday School."

"I *have* taught Sunday School," she replied, keeping her voice calm, "but that has nothing to do with the subject at hand."

An icy chill blew into the room as she felt Sean sizing her up in a new perspective. "I'll teach you how to mix a drink, and I know you'll like it. It's my favorite."

He rose from his desk to go to the bar, obviously expecting her to follow, which she did hesitantly. Following his instructions, she mixed the drink, and handed it to him, but she refused to pour one for herself.

"Suit yourself," he said sharply, visibly perturbed at his inability to convince her. "But I suggest you reconsider. Surely you're aware of the caliber of your job position. My uncle is extremely influential in this city, and should you be unable to handle this job, you may have trouble finding another." His eyes narrowed as he measured her reaction to his remarks.

Kassie had come across rattlesnakes hiding under rocks with more sensitivity than this guy had. "Really, Mr. Phipps, what on earth does drinking have to do with my being able to handle this job?"

"Competency hinges on ability to fit in with the ways of an organization. There's no place here for outmoded puritanical fantasies." The young executive gave her a few more curt instructions and then dismissed her to return to her own office.

Kassie worried over the problem that evening and

wished she had someone to talk to about it. Leomia had gone home early, though, and Glorene was tied up on the phone all evening. Her sense of loneliness was only worsened by the sharp awareness that this was an alien world she'd come to, a world where she felt defenseless and weak. She knew how men like Mr. Phipps were handled back home. She had no idea how to handle the situation here.

She tried to think what Grandpa would tell her to do. But all she could think of was the verse he had always been quoting: "God's grace is sufficient."

Thinking of Grandpa brought burning tears to her eyes as she lay in the darkness of her room that night. "Your grace was sufficient for Grandpa, Lord," she whispered into her pillow. "I know it's sufficient for me too. Give me a heart to run the race with patience."

The next morning a bitter March wind ripped at tatters of gray clouds and chilled Kassie through her all-weather coat as she waited at the bus stop. Not only the wind, but her sister's words from earlier that morning caused a chill in her bones. Once again, Glorene had insisted upon paying for cab fare, but Kassie had stood her ground. "For the price of a cab," she had said stiffly, "I could just as well stay home."

With exasperation, Glorene had snapped back, "What is your problem? Pride, or plain old Carver stubbornness? I'm just trying to help you and you won't accept it. I don't understand you at all."

Now, sitting on the bus stop bench in the spitting rain, Kassie questioned her motives. Was she wrong in her stand? "Lord," she muttered as the bus whined to a stop before her, "could you show Glorene how to help me without smothering me?"

Kassie was in her office, combing out her wet hair, when Wendy walked in. "What happened between you and dear Sean yesterday?" she asked. The friendliness of the previous day had dimmed. "He was mad as a she-bear after working with you. He gave all of us a hard time and nearly fired one of the clerks. Put the poor girl in tears."

"Oh no!" Kassie was stunned. "All I did was refuse a drink. I didn't mean to get his dander up."

"Please," Wendy said, not bothering to veil her sarcasm, "don't try to be a saint at our expense. We don't appreciate it and you won't get a medal for it. Take a couple of sips to please him and pour the rest in a file drawer, but for Pete's sake, get along with him. When you play queen of the Good Ship Lollipop, you rock the boat for the rest of us."

"I *am* sorry, Wendy. I like it here and I want to stay. Perhaps Sean has forgotten all about it. It's a new day." Rain pelted against the high rise windows in defiance of her optimism.

Kassie felt Wendy studying her closely. "Don't count on it," she said, and turned to go, closing the door behind her.

This was unbelievable. What a spoiled brat Sean must be. He didn't get his own way, so he took it out on the other employees. Kassie walked to the windows and stared out at the gray day. What a crazy dilemma.

A sound behind her made her whirl around. "Sean! You scared me half silly." He'd silently entered the room. Perhaps he wasn't like a rattler after all. At least they gave warning.

He walked toward where she was standing. "Kassie, I feel I need to apologize for yesterday. It was childish to get in a huff over such a small matter. From now on, I'll require you to serve drinks for the clients, but you need not join in. Sound reasonable?"

Kassie released a sigh. She ventured a smile, still uncomfortable at his nearness. "I think I can handle that. Thanks."

"See? I'm not such a bad guy, am I?" Sean placed his hand against the window frame behind her, letting his arm lay lightly across her shoulder. With his free hand, he lifted her chin and drew his face near. "Now, let's start all over, you and I. How about it? I'm going to be very easy to get along with. Very easy."

Kassie's reflexes went taut. With quick agility, she ducked to pull away, but she wasn't quick enough. He grabbed her arm and held it tightly. His face reddened as he flared at her, "*Now* what's wrong? Am I poison or something? You sure are the pompous one!"

She struggled against his grip. "Let me go! I came here to work, not to be your plaything."

"A plaything, huh?" He gave a derisive little laugh. "What makes you think I'd even want you for a plaything?" He pressed her to his chest and moved to place his lips upon her. Kassie's hand flew up to push him from her and raked a scratch across his cheek. He swore under his breath and pushed her away in anger.

She was shaken at having hurt him. Indignantly, he touched the scratch and looked at the blood on his fingertips. "All right, Miss Purity, you're going to pay for this."

His tone sent tremors of fear all through her. He left the room, and presently Ed Quillian requested her to report to his office. Briefly, he explained that they had made a mistake in hiring her and that she was being released.

"I know my work has been acceptable," she protested. "Why am I being let go?"

"Young lady, ever since Sean Quillian Phipps was a small boy, he's been groomed to function as head of this business. I accept his opinion that you're not suitable. It's as simple as that. We'll mail your check."

And it *was* as simple as that. As she gathered her things and passed the receptionist's desk, Wendy said, "It's just as well. You've got the guy tearing around here like a two-year-old with a temper tantrum. Why not apply somewhere as a church secretary? You'd be better off."

Kassie mumbled something about being glad to have met her and left. By the time a bus came by, she was wet and chilled once again. Dejectedly, she sat down in the half-empty bus and fought back hot tears.

Passing by Mom Tinsley's apartment house, she felt a cold knot form in the pit of her stomach. The rent sign was gone.

"Oh, Grandpa," she whispered, causing steam to form on the dirty bus window, "why couldn't you have let me stay back in Wyoming where I belong?"

five

Kassie's hand trembled as she fumbled with the lock on the apartment door and let her dripping self inside. She was further distressed to find Glorene in the front room surrounded by a cluster of questioning newsmen.

Glorene looked up at her with genuine concern. "Excuse me a moment, gentlemen," she said. "My sister must be ill to be home at this time of day."

The men continued firing questions regarding Hollister's campaign. Glorene ignored them as she ushered Kassie somewhat brusquely into the kitchen.

"I wasn't ready for the vultures to know who you are, Baby. They could give you a hard time, being my sister. You look terrible. Are you sick?"

In a motherly fashion, Glorene slid the rain bonnet from Kassie's hair, and the gentle touch was enough to make Kassie melt under the weight of her mounting discouragement. Tears rolled down her cheeks, mingling with the rain on her face. "Why didn't you call me to come and get you?" Glorene questioned.

"I've been fired. I no longer work for the ad agency." She sunk into a chair as droplets soaked into the lemon carpet.

"Fired? That's impossible. The job couldn't have been *that* hard. Where's the foul up?"

Glorene's sharp retort reminded Kassie that she'd get no true motherly concern from her sister. Glorene was no doubt anxious to get back to the newsmen who were waiting.

"Sean Phipps stepped out of line and made a pass at me," Kassie said softly, straining to stop the trembling. "When I resisted, he threw a fit and had his uncle fire me."

"A pass?"

"He tried to kiss me."

Glorene shook her head. "You should be so lucky. That Sean is a knockout. I've seen him. You could have humored him a little."

Kassie stiffened. "No man is going to touch me until I'm equally as ready as he is. I'm not some mountain windflower to be plucked at someone's whim."

"Sounds a little snobbish to me." Glorene stood and drew a slender cigarette package from the pocket of her gaily-flowered hostess gown. "For your information, when I learned you had a job there, I planned a dinner party for Saturday evening with Sean as one of the guests. I had hoped you could help Creighton and me with a little behind-the-scenes diplomatic work. But now your lily-white principles have thrown a wrench in the works."

Thoughtfully, Glorene tapped the cigarette against the package, then lit it. "You don't *have* to work at the agency, I suppose. I could find someone else to do that part. But you'd better take advantage of Saturday night to mend your broken fences with Sean or you'll cause me some bad trouble. After all, you do owe me a little, you know."

Glorene blew a silvery curl of smoke in the air and added, "You don't need to work anyway. I'll take good care of you. Now get into some dry clothes and don't worry about a silly little job. I've got to get back out there and feed the vultures."

Kassie sat very still for a time before rising and walking through the breakfast alcove to her room. Her mind was a fog. She remembered Loren's kiss the week before. She hadn't scratched him. And the only fighting she had done was fighting to keep from falling completely into his embrace. Did that mean she had been ready? And willing? What did it all mean?

Her only wish was that she'd listened to that uneasy feeling she'd had about Quillian's the very first day. That small still Voice, the one she had thought she'd learned to hear and obey, had been speaking to her, but she hadn't listened.

The remainder of the week dragged by. Kassie ignored Glorene's statement about not looking for work. She continued to follow up on interview appointments, but nothing materialized. Had she been jobless back in Cody, she would have hired on as a waitress until something better came along. But Glorene would have a fit. "We've got to think of the press now," she kept saying.

On Friday afternoon, Kassie stepped out into the sunshine and ventured in a new direction from the apartment to take a long walk. In the back of her mind, the thought of the Saturday night party loomed before her. How she dreaded facing Sean again.

Through the afternoon, she window shopped, but made no purchases. On the way home, she saw ahead of her a massive buff brick building with the name McKinley Memorial Hospital on the front. She smiled as she squinted up at it.

This could be the answer to her problem of too much idle time. With new enthusiasm, she pushed through the revolving doors and asked if they needed any volunteer help.

A girl just younger than herself, dressed in pink, sat at the information desk. "We always need volunteers," she said, pulling a form from the desk and handing it to Kassie. "What hours could you work?"

"Oh, all day!" Kassie answered quickly, brightening at the thought of being useful once again. "And evenings too. Until I find a full-time job, that is."

"Wait a minute." The dark-haired girl laughed easily. "We wouldn't want you to burn out the first week. Some patients can be pretty cantankerous."

"I guess I sound over-anxious, don't I? But I do have extra time on my hands. I took care of my invalid grandfather for two years before he died, so I understand some of the frustrations of being bedfast."

"I see," said the girl, combing fingers through her short curly hair. "I'm Holly Henman. Why don't you fill out these forms and stop by Monday morning? We'll fit you with a uniform and assign your hours then. What's your name?"

"I'm Kassie Carver. Please, couldn't I visit someone now? I've nothing else to do, and I'd only take a minute."

This was what she needed to get her mind off the loss of her job and the upcoming party. Reaching out to someone else never failed to work whenever she became too wrapped up in her own problems.

Holly studied her for a moment. "I see no reason why not. Follow me."

Antiseptic odors were strong outside the darkened room on the eighth floor where Holly led Kassie. She could barely make out the form lying in the bed, face to the wall.

"A case of too much liquor and self-pity," whispered Holly as they stood together outside the door. "She has physical problems as well which are being treated, but that's certainly not the whole picture. She's been a real challenge to us, Kassie. No one can reach her. Her family seldom comes, and when they do, she screams at them unmercifully."

"How dreadful." Kassie longed to draw open the drapes and let the sunlight banish the oppression from the room.

"I'll leave you alone with Lexi." Holly patted her shoulder. "The doctors say a short visit is best."

Kassie breathed a silent prayer before stepping inside. "Lexi? Hello there. My name's Kassie Carver and I've come for a visit. I'm so glad winter's over and spring has arrived, aren't you? I saw a fat robin in the park earlier today, gathering bits of thread to build a nest. I thought of the beauty of God's plan to place that instinct of nest-building within every robin. God's creations are wonderful, aren't they?"

As she spoke, Kassie placed her purse on a chair, and busied herself about the room, tidying things up. She noticed that several of the potted plants were dry. They were in dire need of sunshine as well as water.

Rummaging in her purse, she pulled out her small Bible. "May I read to you, Lexi? I'd like to share my favorite Psalm, but I'll have to turn on this small lamp so I can see the words."

Kassie thought she detected a slight movement beneath the covers. The hair that peeped out showed signs of graying. Kassie turned her eyes back to the page. "Whither shall I go from thy spirit? or whither shall I flee from thy presence?. . .thy hand lead me, and thy right hand shall hold me."

The Psalm was comforting to Kassie as she read, helping her to forget the loss of her job and the mistreatment from Glorene.

"How precious also are thy thoughts unto me, O God! how great is the sum of them! If I should count them, they are more in number than the sand..."

A scratchy voice from beneath the covers scoffed, "No one can count the sand. That's impossible."

Kassie straightened in her chair. "That's right. That's precisely what the psalmist meant. We can't number the sand nor can we number God's thoughts toward us. We're *always* in His thoughts. Isn't that wonderful?"

In the dim light, Kassie saw a tired and weary, though not unattractive, face staring at her with red-rimmed eyes.

"And you're just a child," Lexi continued bitterly, "what would you know about God? What could you know about *life* for that matter?"

"God makes provision for youth to know Him as well as older people," Kassie assured her. "And as for life, Jesus is the Way, the Truth and the *Life*."

The older woman let her head fall back on the pillow. "Trite clichés," she said with a deep sigh. "How I weary of them. Everyone who comes in here thinks he has the perfect answer. Who are you and why have you come?"

"I've signed to be a volunteer, but I didn't want to wait until Monday to help. I wanted to reach out to someone today."

"Oh, the hollow wind of youthful zeal. Such a waste. I suppose they sent you up here thinking fresh troops would do the trick. The connivers!"

Kassie ignored the negative remarks and ventured to

point out to Lexi the dying plants which needed light and water.

"Let them die!" the woman snapped, her face becoming twisted and white. "Why should they flourish while I wither away? And if you touch those drapes, I'll scream!"

"I won't open the drapes until you tell me to," Kassie answered in a steady voice. "And I won't even read to you unless you ask me. Will that be all right?" She had thought at first she was making progress, but now she wasn't sure.

Somewhat appeased, the woman's face relaxed again. "That's better."

"You have attractive eyes, Lexi. And such a clear lovely complexion. As soon as you feel up to it, perhaps I could give your hair a fussy do and put on a bit of makeup to pretty you up for your family."

"My family hates me."

"In that case, you may want to do it only to please yourself."

"We'll see." Suspicion lingered in her voice. "You're coming back?"

"On Monday," Kassie assured her. "If I'm not assigned to your floor, I'll make a special point to stop by anyway."

"I don't need your pity." The dejected patient had once more turned her head away.

Kassie reached out and softly touched the shoulder covered in blankets. "I meant I'd *want* to come and see you, Lexi. I'd better go and let you rest. 'Bye now."

She received no answer.

Back at the first floor desk, Kassie reported to Holly. "Lexi's a bit snippy, but we got along fine."

Holly looked up from her paper work. "Snippy? She spoke to you?"

Kassie nodded.

"That lady has spoken to no volunteer since she was admitted more than a week ago. Wait until her doctor hears about this."

Her plan had worked. Kassie's thoughts were now filled with prayer and concern for Lexi, and Monday morning held in store something other than idle time. As she stood before her closet Saturday evening, studying her wardrobe, she felt relaxed and refreshed.

Only one dress hung on the rod that was even moderately formal. From what Glorene had said, Kassie supposed that was what was expected. She pulled out the simple black velvet trimmed with white lace at the throat and sleeves. It would have to do.

"Lord," she whispered as she brushed her dark hair into an upsweep, "it's a mystery to me how I can please Glorene and still please You as well. Help me to be sociable to Sean Phipps without making a terrible scene."

As she looked out, guests were already milling throughout the large baroque-styled room, which was adorned with wicker-colored brocade draperies. The subdued colors of the room were overpowered by the vivid hues of formal dresses worn by attending guests.

Kassie slipped back into the kitchen to see if Leomia needed any help.

"Silly girl. You belong out there." Leomia nodded her head toward the noisy crowd. "You look so lovely." The hand that gently touched Kassie's cheek smelled heavily of foodstuffs. "So different from your sister, yet so like her," Leomia murmured, half to herself. "Now, Kassie, remember—just because Glorene says things real loud don't mean she's convinced she's right. You gotta live your life too. Stand up for what you know is right."

Kassie was grateful for the brief words of encouragement. Before she could answer, Glorene spotted her and rushed toward her with a rustling of her salmon-colored satin dress. "Kassie, come and meet our guests." Stepping closer, she whispered, "What did you think this was, a funeral? If I'd known you didn't have something colorful to wear, I'd have loaned you a dress."

Kassie drew in a short breath. "My dress is fine, and I'm comfortable."

"Oh, never mind." Glorene gave an impatient wave, then drew her through the crowd with exchanges of meaningless conversation, introducing her here and there. Finally, she was deposited with a group of elderly dowagers with whom she had nothing in common. As soon as was politely possible, she slipped from their midst and migrated toward the terrace door to catch a breath of air.

Involuntarily, she found herself watching for Loren's appearance, then chided herself. After all, she'd not even heard if he was to be present.

"Kassie?"

Startled, she turned to see Sean standing near her. The old sparkle was in his eyes, and he gave her a roguish smile. He must have sensed her shrinking back.

"Don't panic," he said and waggled both hands in a gesture of surrender, then slowly placed them behind his back. "No touch. No kidding. Will you come out on the terrace? I'd like to talk to you."

She still felt no trust for this man, but she would humor him for Glorene's sake. Surely with a roomful of guests nearby...

"Say," he began, as the cool night air caressed their

faces, "you might have told a fellow you were Glorene Paquette's sister."

"And why should the identity of my kin make any difference?"

"You're right, of course." His smile fled. He seemed uncomfortable. She wondered if it were a new emotion to him. "I don't even know how to ask you to forgive me," he said with a shrug. "I've never known a girl like you— one who can't be swayed."

Kassie sat down at the wrought iron table and looked up to where Sean was leaning against the terrace railing. A slight breeze from the bay ruffled his sandy hair. She marveled at the boyish features of his ruddy cheeks. But the childish side of him, the spoiled and pampered side of him, was a tiger.

"I acted irrationally in asking Uncle Ed to fire you because I was humiliated. I deserved the scratch." He rubbed the red mark on his cheek. "I thought sure you would crumple when I threatened to blacklist you, but you never wavered." He shook his head. "Come back to work for me, will you, please? I'll raise your salary and I'll leave you alone. I truly want you as my secretary, Kassie. Truly."

Kassie turned away from the pleading eyes and tried to collect her thoughts. What would Glorene want her to do? What was expected of her now? But Leomia's words came back to her and helped her make up her mind.

"No, I think not." She smoothed the lap of the soft velvet dress. "It's a generous offer, but I was wrong to accept the position in the first place. Your agency is not where the Lord would have me be right now."

Sean's face registered his puzzlement. "The Lord? What does He...?" The unfinished question dangled in the night air. "You're a wonderful girl. Will you at least give me the opportunity to win back your respect? May I see you again?"

She could not calculate Sean's full sincerity. He was obviously in the habit of getting his own way, and she had no way to predict what theatrics he might stoop to.

"I'll consider it and let you know." His brashness was still fresh in her mind.

Sean moved from the railing and placed his hand over hers on the tabletop. "I'll give you time. I'll call you next week."

She withdrew her hand and stood. "We'd better go in. I'm getting chilled."

He did not so much as touch her arm as they returned undetected into the crowd. Undetected, that is, except to one person.

"Kassie, there you are."

"Loren!" Her breath caught in her throat at the sight of him dressed in a pale blue suit nearly the color of his eyes, his face looking burnished and strong.

Loren sent a curious glance over her head at Sean, realizing they had come in from the terrace together.

"I don't believe we've met," Sean said. He seemed to be enjoying the fact that he'd aroused Loren's curiosity. "But I recognize you, Mr. Marcellus. I'm Sean Quillian Phipps."

Loren returned Sean's handshake. Looking back at Kassie, he asked, "Isn't that the firm you're working for? Quillian's?"

Kassie felt the warmth rising to her cheeks. She didn't know how to answer with Sean at her elbow. "Yes," she began. "I was hired last Monday, but..."

Sean broke in with a carefree laugh, "You know the story of Little Miss Muffet, don't you, Marcellus? That old spider was only being himself, but he frightened her away. Well, I was being myself, in tune with my own nature, and I frightened Miss Muffet away." He waved a hand toward Kassie.

"I see," Loren replied slowly.

"And now," Sean continued, "the bad old spider is out to mend his ways."

Kassie was not amused by this ridiculous conversation and once again felt she was being treated as a nonentity. She was thankful, however, that she'd not been pressed to explain the mess to Loren.

Done with listening, Loren took her arm. "If you'd like, I'll find you something to drink, then I must tell you what Jolly Roger did for me today."

Had she been asked, Kassie would have been hard pressed to explain why she'd resisted Sean so firmly, then passively allowed the broad-shouldered Loren to steer her through the crowded room to the refreshment table.

Sean's eyes narrowed as he watched them go.

six

The phone was ringing when Kassie stepped into the apartment after church the next morning. She was humming strains of "How Great Thou Art." It had been Grandpa's favorite hymn, and it still echoed in her mind from the church service.

Kassie assumed Glorene was in her room and would answer the jangling phone. It rang several times before Kassie finally realized she was alone and grabbed at the phone on the marble-topped coffee table.

Exhilarated from the stirring church service and quiet walk home in the spring sunshine, she gave a bright hello.

"You're sounding mighty chipper this morning," came Sean's voice over the line. "Where've you been? I've tried to reach you for over an hour."

"It's Sunday. I was in church."

"Church. Of course! Silly of me not to have thought of that."

Unsure as to the reason for his call, Kassie hoped he would get to the point and let her go.

"Have you had lunch?" he asked.

"I just now walked in the door."

"I'll bet you're famished. I'll pick up some sandwiches and be there in a flash. Have you seen the Ronson Gardens?"

"No I haven't, but..."

"It's a must-see for every newcomer to Westport. It's

only about five miles up the coast. You like flowers, don't you?"

"Who doesn't like flowers?"

"And gardens?"

"Yes..."

"Say no more, Kassie. I'll be there in one fleeting moment of time, and we'll see the gardens together. Some of the early flowers will be in bloom."

Her encounters with the young Mr. Phipps had been anything but pleasant, and now he was suggesting they spend time together. Kassie wasn't sure. She'd heard about the botanical gardens and wanted to see them, but she'd decided to do so when she had more time and money of her own.

"I know what you're thinking," Sean was saying in a more gentle tone. "And I can't blame you one bit for not trusting me. But I know you're fair—and you're not above giving a person a second chance. Did you have other plans for the afternoon?"

Other plans? If he only knew what a joke that was. "No," she told him. "No other plans."

"It's settled then. I'll be there in twenty minutes."

Slowly, she replaced the receiver. *How crazy.* How could she allow herself to go out with Sean after he had treated her so rudely and caused her to be fired? And yet he had sounded sincere at the party when he'd offered her the job back again. Perhaps he was having second thoughts about his actions. If so, she couldn't keep clinging to an old grudge.

She pushed open the french doors and stepped into the fresh breeze. In the hazy distance she could see brightly striped sails scooting along the sun-spangled waters of the bay. In the short time she had been here, she had become hopelessly smitten with this ocean front, and yet she hadn't spent a moment on the beach. Glorene's interests were not in that direction—unless, of course, some waterfront property was for sale.

Twenty minutes! Sean would be there in twenty minutes and here she stood daydreaming. Quickly she hurried to her room and pulled out a scoop-neck cotton dress in aqua, while wondering if slacks would be a wiser choice. Just as she was tying the rope belt and slipping into her sandals, the doorbell rang. She took just a moment to run the brush through her hair, realizing the futility of her efforts. After all, the breeze would be brisk out there by the water. She tossed the brush back on her dresser and ran to get the door.

Sean's ruddy face was all smiles. His appearance was altered, dressed in casual clothes rather than a suit. Cordially, he greeted her, and with only a touch on her arm, guided her through the doorways and into his car.

The sleek little white sports convertible was exactly the type of car she could have predicted he would own. She smelled the aroma of the sandwiches lying in a sack in the back seat, and she realized she was hungry.

"The gardens aren't in full bloom yet," he said as he maneuvered the small racy car in and out of the traffic heading out of town. "But then, there aren't as many tourists yet either. I've always felt that to see the gardens in all seasons is to appreciate the peak blossom season even more. I even come out here on cold winter days."

This definitely was not the same man who had acted the fool at the Quillian Ad Agency last week, and long before they reached the garden entrance, she found herself relaxing in his presence, sharing with him about her life in Wyoming and how much she missed it.

Sean purchased soft drinks at the concession stand near the Ronson Gardens entrance, and then put an area map in her hand. "There are backwater inlets with cypress trees and a wilderness garden setting," he explained, pointing to the map. "Up here are the formal gardens and the open beaches. Which would you prefer?"

Kassie thought for a moment. She wanted to see it all, but obviously they wouldn't have time. "Which do you like best?"

"The beach, definitely."

"The beach it is then," she said with a smile.

Their walk led them through the well-defined paths of a formal garden, set in stringent, disciplined geometric patterns. It was as Sean had said, for she could hardly wait to come back and see the dogwood, roses, camellias, and azaleas after they had exploded into blossoms. Already, entire banks of jonquils nodded their pretty yellow heads at them. Fat waxy buds on the magnolia trees were beginning to swell.

Brisk salt water air greeted them through the tall formal shrubbery as they strolled along side by side. Sean turned off the path and led her up the steps into a lacy gazebo covered with trailing wisteria vines.

"Hungry?"

"As you said on the phone—famished!"

With great decorum, he set out the drinks and pulled from the sack neatly wrapped ham and cheese sandwiches. "I didn't ask," he said, laughing. "I simply assume everyone likes what I like. More evidence of the spoiled kid that I am. Right?"

"Ham and cheese is fine," she assured him, thinking she was hungry enough to eat the wrappings. "Do you mind if I offer a word of thanks to the Giver of these goodies before we devour them?"

Sean looked at her for a moment. "Sure. Why not?"

He didn't tease as she bowed her head and blessed their picnic lunch. Afterward, she asked, "If you're not comfortable with the image of the spoiled Quillian heir, why not change the image?"

"How do you propose I do that? By attaching myself to some of your beliefs about church and alcoholic abstinence? I hardly see how that could change one's personality." Sean's fair hair glinted in the afternoon sunlight as he shook his head. "No. I'm afraid religion isn't the answer for my life. You can't understand the pressures of being the only living male relative of Ed Quillian and the son of his dear sister Edith."

"The character of a Christian needn't be something tacked on," she explained between bites. "It's an outgrowth of an inner changing. It comes from allowing the One who created us to be the Lord within us."

"I have enough people 'lording' over me, thank you very much. Between Mother and Uncle Ed, they do quite well. Too well, in fact." Sean gave a hearty laugh at his pun. His laughter was nice, she had to admit, and it made the afternoon seem suddenly very bright. Kassie couldn't help but think if his mother were anything like his Uncle Ed, Sean did have his share of problems.

When they finished eating, Sean took her by the hand and pulled her along as they easily ran through the rest of the walkways. She was laughing breathlessly when suddenly the thick masses of trees and shrubs of the garden broke open onto the white beach. Still holding tightly to her hand, he led her, not so fast now, down the shallow steps and onto the sand.

Kassie stared at the swell and curl of each foamy little wave that crept in upon the sand. She gave a squeal as Sean led her across the broad beach right out to the water's edge. She was not prepared for the immensity of the ocean's horizon.

He led her along the edge of the tiny waves. "Want to take your sandals off?" he asked.

"Oh, yes." Hurriedly, she pulled them off and let the waves sweep gently over the tops of her feet. She dug her toes into the tight wet sand. Sean pulled off his sandals as well and rolled up his pant legs. They strolled along leisurely, talking about mundane things. Mostly, Kassie simply gazed at the delicious sight of the mammoth ocean and the perfect line of the horizon.

At one point, she stopped to shade her eyes with her hands. Her heart was overflowing with the beauty that surrounded her. "'How precious also are thy thoughts unto me O God!'" she quoted almost without thinking. "'If I should count them, they are more in number than the sand.' More than all the sand. The mind can hardly conceive it." She knelt down to scoop a little hole in the sand, and watched as a wave first filled it, then smoothed it out as the water rushed back out to sea.

"I suppose it gives a person some degree of comfort to recite the Psalms like that," Sean remarked. "The human psyche is prone to lean on such buffers against the forces of day-to-day life."

Kassie glanced up at him. "And how, pray tell, did you know I was quoting from the Psalms?"

Sean's face broke into a boyish grin. "My great-grandmother used to read to me from the Psalms. When I was very small, before I ever started to go to school."

"Oh, really?" She rose to her feet. "Her human psyche leaned on the Scriptures, did it?"

He paused. "You know, I think Grandma actually believed it all. Strange," he added.

"Not so strange, Mr. Phipps. My psyche leans on the Scriptures, and my psyche, my mind, and my heart believe every word!"

"Imagination is a powerful force. Great men through the ages have proven that. If you want to believe in the Bible, then for you, it's real."

Kassie had heard enough. She detested debating away the simplistic beauty of God's Word. Suddenly, without warning, she went racing through the shallow waves, delighting at the splashing against her legs, mindless that the skirt of her dress was getting soaked. And she had thought horseback riding was exciting? As she ran, she became in tune with the rhythmic, rolling waves, the gleaming sandy beaches, and the endless stretch of open sky.

"Hey!" Sean yelled from behind her. "You're faster than a wild pony. Wait up." With an effort, he eventually caught up, grabbed her hand, and steered her toward the grassy dunes, pulling her down beside him. Their laughter together was pleasant on the air.

"Old slow poke," she teased.

"Slow poke?" he retorted. "I'll have you know you're talking to a perpetual jogger here. I never miss a day."

She laughed again. "Isn't doing you much good. You need to stop jogging and start running," she teased.

"You just got a head start."

She squeezed water from the tail of her skirt and flicked it on him. "Head start, my foot. I won fair and square. 'Fess up."

Sean sprawled out on the sand, leaning back on his elbows as he looked at her. "Yeah, you did." He paused, staring at her. "You're an exciting woman, Kassie. And beautiful as well."

For the first time that day, the familiar feeling of discomfort returned. She gave a slight laugh. "Because I can run faster than you?"

His gaze was steady. "You know that's not what I meant."

As though for the first time, Kassie looked full into Sean's face and saw past the façade of the pampered young corporate executive on his way to the top. "I'm not sure *what* you meant. But I accept your compliment and thank you for it."

"Will you let me see you again?"

"I don't think I can answer that now." She dug her fingers through the warm soft sand and pulled up a small, curious-looking shell and studied it. "Will you give me time to think about it and not push me?"

"I've seen where pushing gets me. I promise not to do that again." Sean sat upright. Their shoulders were touching. "Take this little shell home with you," he instructed. "Place it on your dresser to remind you that Sean Quillian Phipps was a perfect gentleman for one entire day. A feat that is greater than you may ever know or fully appreciate." He leaned closer and touched her forehead with one soft kiss.

"I will, Sean. And thanks for showing me the gardens.

They're more lovely than I ever imagined they could be." She slipped the shell into the pocket of her dress. "We'd better go. It's getting late."

Without argument, he stood and gave her a hand up. Together, their silence comfortable, they walked back through the gardens to the parking lot.

After the drive back to the city, Sean never asked Kassie if he could walk her up to the apartment. He simply found a parking place nearly a block away and got out of his car. As they came to the apartment entrance, he never let go of her hand. Laughing, they stepped out of the elevator at her floor—and ran smack into Loren Marcellus.

"Loren!" Kassie sucked in a gasp of surprise.

Loren stepped back and stared. Kassie's hair was a shambles, her skirt was wrinkled from having been wet, and she was still carrying her sandals.

"Hello, Marcellus," Sean said coolly. "Looking for someone?"

Loren's clear eyes studied them through a chilly silence before he said to Kassie, "Glorene's been trying to call you all afternoon. She was beginning to worry. She asked me to stop by and check on you. I'm sure she had no idea you were in such good hands."

"Good hands to be sure," Sean said, raising his hands with one still clasped onto Kassie's.

"I left a note," Kassie explained. "I guess she's not been back since this morning."

"She's at campaign headquarters," Loren said. "She's been there all day working with Hollister and the others. By the way, Creighton wants to talk with you next week. Is there a day when you'll be free?"

"Me? Whatever for?"

"Something about some work he wants done."

"But I know nothing about politics."

"The political system is simple, Kassie," Sean broke in. "Whoever has the most money buys the most influence. The highest amount of pressure wins the election."

Loren carefully ignored Sean. "He didn't say it had anything to do with the campaign. Will you see him or not?"

Kassie felt herself pulling back. If this was something Glorene had set up, she wanted nothing to do with it. The puppet strings of her sister's manipulation were pulling too tight lately. Loren loomed tall before her, waiting for an answer. "I'm doing some volunteer work on Monday," she began.

"Tuesday morning then? Hollister could see you at about ten."

What she'd heard about Southerners moving slowly wasn't true. On the contrary, the ones she'd met moved quickly and dragged her along in their wake. "Tuesday will be fine, I suppose. How do I find his office?"

"I'll pick you up. I told him I would." He moved toward the elevator.

"Thanks for stopping by," she said.

"Thank your sister. *She* was concerned." He poked at the elevator button and then stepped in without another word.

Sean tugged at her hand and led her down the hall toward the apartment. "Intense guy, isn't he?"

"I guess you could say that," she mumbled, digging the keys from the bottom of her purse. She could see no reason for Loren to be so short with her. What was he upset about now? This time he had no horse or dog to blame his anger on.

Kassie was grateful that Sean retained his manners and did not ask to come in the apartment. Suddenly, she felt leaden and wanted to lie down. Perhaps it was the sea air. But she was also disturbed at Loren's aloof manner. How different from the night he'd brought her home. Perhaps he was just a moody guy.

"Thanks for trusting me," Sean was saying. "I'll call you next week. There's so much of the gardens we didn't see..."

She didn't let him finish. "It *was* a wonderful day. Thanks for everything. We'll make further plans next week." And she gently but firmly closed the door.

Her note to Glorene still lay on the table in the hall. She wadded it up and dropped it into the trash basket in her room. She pampered herself with a warm tub soak and a good shampoo to get rid of all the sand and grit of the day. She devoured a sandwich and a few of Leomia's famous oatmeal cookies, certain that once she crawled into bed, sleep would come instantaneously.

The shrill ring of the phone shattered her calm. If that was Glorene wanting her to do something or go someplace...

"Hello?"

"Kassie? Sorry to bother you so late. This is Loren."

seven

Kassie propped herself up on one elbow and pushed her dark hair back from her eyes. "Yes, Loren?" She was helpless to keep the irritation from sounding in her voice. "What is it?" What had he forgotten to tell her? More directions from Glorene and Creighton? Perhaps he was checking to see if she had actually gotten to bed on time. Muffling a yawn, she reached out to switch on the lamp. Eleven-thirty and still Glorene had not come in. Natty was curled up asleep on her chaise, which he often did when Glorene was gone.

"Did I wake you?"

"Heavens, no. I was lying here waiting to see who would call me after eleven at night."

"You *were* asleep."

"It's been a long day."

"But a *good* day. Right?"

Kassie fluffed the pillows up behind her back as a dozen prickly questions filled her fuzzy brain. "Well, yes, it was. I was able to walk along a sandy beach and dip my toes in genuine ocean waves for the first time since arriving at Westport. I fell in love with it."

"Ever ridden horseback along a beach?" Loren asked.

What was this? She slowly came more fully awake. "Considering that today was the first day I've ever been on a beach in my life, I guess the answer would be no. Did you call this late to discuss various methods for

72

enjoying beaches?"

"Anyone who loves horses as much as you do could never fully experience the coastal areas until you've discovered it on horseback. You can ride the trails up around Weller's Cove. It's gorgeous there."

"Really? I can't imagine any place more lovely than Ronson Gardens." Was this an invitation or was he merely giving information? At least his sharp attitude from earlier in the day had softened. For that she was thankful.

"You'll understand what I mean when you see it. Before long, the gardens will be riddled with noisy, nosey tourists poking around, but the Coves are secluded. Hidden away."

"Sounds very mysterious." Kassie twisted the coil of the phone cord around her fingers. Surely he'd get to the point in a moment and let her get back to sleep.

"Kassie? About this afternoon..."

"Yes?"

"I wanted to call and apologize for being so abrupt with you. I was more than a little surprised to see you with Phipps."

"Surprised?" She'd never have guessed that Loren Marcellus would be looking out for her interests. Counting Glorene, Kassie mused, that made two people who thought they knew what was best for her. "Why should you be surprised? Didn't you hear Glorene say she wanted me to help pull in new recruits?"

"You wouldn't do that—even if Glorene ordered it. You're not the type."

Kassie gave a wry little laugh. "Thanks for your vote of confidence."

"Are you accepting my apology or not? It seems you were easier to apologize to the last time."

"Perhaps you should stop doing things for which you'll be sorry—then you wouldn't have to ask."

"Look, Miss Muffet, I just didn't like the thought of the spider coming back disguised as a friendly butterfly. I've heard of Sean's reputation in Westport. It's common knowledge."

"I see. And how well do you know Sean personally? Perhaps all the talk is exaggerated." From the bedside table she took the iridescent shell and fingered its smoothness. She was becoming convinced Sean's reputation was not at all indicative of his true personality. She disliked Glorene ordering her to humor him, but on the other hand, she certainly didn't need any of Loren's warnings either.

Loren's end was quiet for a moment. *Rethinking his words, perhaps?* "I know him well enough," he said. "Just consider yourself warned by a friend and we'll let it go at that."

"How about if I agree to keep a fly swatter handy? In case the butterfly turns pesky."

"Very funny."

"Oh, and I do accept your apology."

"Finally?"

"Given time, I usually come through."

"I'll see you Tuesday morning at nine o'clock sharp," Loren conveniently changed the subject. "Be ready."

"If Glorene's here, she'll insist on taking me."

"Glorene's going out of town on a scouting job for Hollister."

How nice to learn such news secondhand. "Really? Then I'll see you Tuesday morning at nine o'clock sharp. And don't be late," she said in a mocking tone.

"Very funny."

"Thanks for calling."

"Good night, Kassie."

The same feelings that had haunted her the night he'd brought her home from the Rhapsody Club were surging and swirling deep inside her. She was a little bewildered, though; why should he care who she was with and what she was doing? Did she appear that empty headed? A small town girl who needed a guardian, is that what Loren Marcellus thought of her? At least she was happy about one thing—he no longer seemed so aloof. On the phone just now, he sounded almost human.

Sleep had fled. She drank a glass of milk and read the entire book of Esther before she regained it.

ᴤ

On Monday morning at McKinley Memorial Hospital, Kassie was issued a trim pink uniform to change into and was sent immediately to the pediatric ward. There she made fast friends with several of the children, including ten-year-old Mindy, a victim of leukemia, who amazed Kassie with her vibrant faith and her knowledge of Scripture. Mindy's bright eyes came alive when she learned that Kassie was also a Christian.

"Wow," she said. "That's really cool. Now we can pray for the other kids together. The Lord must have sent you along to help me."

Kassie laughed. "I'm not sure you need much help at this point, but I'd be happy to join forces with you."

When her time was up in the pediatric ward, she hurried up to the eighth floor to check on Lexi, finding her in a horrendous mood. *What a selfish person,* Kassie thought as she attempted to bridge the ever-widening gap between this woman and the world of reality. But Lexi didn't want to be read to, or even talked to, and she refused to allow the curtains to be opened to let in the glorious light of the spring day.

From Holly's encouraging words on Friday, Kassie had fooled herself into thinking she had made headway with Lexi, when apparently she hadn't after all. After a time of uncomfortable strained silence, Kassie finally said, "I'm leaving now, Lexi. I have an afternoon appointment that I don't want to miss."

Before leaving the apartment that morning, she'd received a call from her employment agency informing her that an afternoon appointment had been scheduled for an interview. "I'll try to get back to see you again as soon as possible."

"You probably didn't want to come in the first place," came the cracked voice from beneath the covers. "And now that you've found I'm no piece of cake you won't want to come back."

Kassie paused a moment. She didn't want to lie, and Lexi was partially right: being with her wasn't a pleasant task. "God's grace is sufficient for me," she said. "And for you as well, if you give Him half a chance. 'Bye now."

Holly looked up as Kassie's steps clicked across the tiled lobby toward her desk. "How'd it go?" she asked.

"It's a strange paradox, Holly. A little girl in the pediatric ward may die, who hasn't lived but a fraction of her life, and she's as full of joy as anyone I've ever met. Then there's the healthy Lexi who could live a full and productive life—but all she wants is to pull the covers over her head and give up on living altogether."

Holly gave a sigh. "I hadn't thought of it quite like that, but it's the truth. Lexi must have given you a bad time today."

"She did. She's built up such a wall of defense."

"Part of that is guilt and shame for humiliating her

family. They're trying to keep the story under wraps. We never give out her real name."

Kassie shook her head. "Good thing I don't know it then. I'm terrible about keeping secrets."

Holly pulled out the time sheets to re-schedule Kassie.

"Better skip tomorrow," Kassie told her. "Something's come up and I don't know how long it will take." Again, she mulled over the message that Creighton wanted to see her. She wished she could refuse to go. She'd much prefer to be at McKinley with Mindy and the other children. "Put me down for Wednesday, all day."

Holly smiled. "You got it."

❧

The job interview that afternoon was a disappointment, as they all had been lately. So many positions required several years of experience, which she sorely lacked. How could a person gain experience, if companies refused to hire for lack of experience?

The gentleman who conducted the interview was pleasant, but not promising. The office was nice, but it was in the heart of the downtown business district. Never yet had she felt comfortable in the downtown area of Westport. Surely she could get used to it, though, if she had to.

Noisy Natty met her at the front door of the apartment and she knew Glorene was home. Pushing the dog away with her foot, Kassie thought if she ever had the opportunity, she'd love to teach the pretty little dog to be quiet and obedient.

Easing the door shut behind her, she could hear Glorene and Leomia talking softly in the kitchen. Tantalizing aromas reminded her that she had bypassed lunch in her busy day.

Sticking her head around the kitchen door, Glorene said,

"There she is. My wayward little sister home at last. I was about to send a search party out for you. Where have you been this time?"

"Volunteer work and job interviews," Kassie answered as she joined them. "Hi, Leomia. What's cooking? It smells wonderful."

"Chicken cacciatore. But you two will have to serve yourselves and clean up the dishes. I'll be leaving early. My little grandbaby is sick and my daughter needs my help. I was just giving Glorene a few last minute instructions."

"She thinks I don't know how to put a dinner on the table—a dinner that she's finished up to the last detail. She treats me like a dummy. You'd think she hired *me* rather than the other way around."

"I didn't say that," Leomia protested with her hands on her ample hips.

"You didn't have to. The insinuation was painful enough. Were you going to lay out the serving spoons, or do you think I can figure that out myself?"

"Glorene Paquette, shame on you!" In exasperation, Leomia threw a damp kitchen towel at her employer, which missed the mark and landed with a splat on the floor.

Glorene gave a soft whistle. "Lucky you didn't have the crock pot in your hand."

"You're so hard-headed, you'd never notice. I don't have time to mess around here. I've got to get going. Please remember to soak the casserole dish, ladies, so I don't get blisters trying to scrub it tomorrow."

Kassie smiled at their friendly bickering. "Guess I'll go change," she excused herself. "See you tomorrow, Leomia."

"By the way," Leomia said, stopping at the door, "did

you get a job?"

"I don't know for sure, but it doesn't look like it."

"Don't worry, you'll find something soon. I'm sure the Lord has something special for you."

"I know. Thanks."

When Kassie came out later from changing, Leomia was gone and Glorene had the table set. The stereo was playing a CD of Broadway tunes. For once Natty was settled down—undisturbed and undisturbing.

The chicken cacciatore, homemade dinner rolls, and Waldorf salad were delectable. Mentally, Kassie made a vow to begin exercising soon. Too much inaction and good food could be a dangerous combination.

Glorene was rather subdued as they ate. Kassie wondered if she should ask about her going away, or wait to see if her sister would bring up the subject herself. Finally, after she'd finished her meal and searched the refrigerator for a carton of raspberry sherbet, Glorene began to relax and loosen up. "I hate heavy desserts," she said, carrying the carton and two stemmed crystal sherbet dishes to the table. "Want some?"

"Love some. Raspberry's my favorite."

"Really?" Her sister seemed as interested as though Kassie had just imparted some important revelation. "Sometimes it's difficult to believe you're my sister since we know so little about one another." She artfully turned up two perfectly rounded scoops of sherbet and served them. "I don't even know what you like and don't like."

If only you'd *listen*, Kassie wanted to shout, that's a surefire way to get to know someone.

"Will you be all right here if I leave for a couple of days?" Glorene asked.

Finally, she was going to mention the trip. "I'll be fine.

Leomia will be around, won't she? Where're you going?"

"Florida. There's a campaign going on down there that Creighton wants me to observe. A clean campaign. That's what Creighton wants." She pushed back her dish. "More?"

Kassie shook her head. "I've never heard of people studying other campaigns. Is that done often?"

"I'm not sure. I'm a little new at all this. But if that's what Creighton wants, then I'll do it."

"You're very fond of him, aren't you?" Kassie ventured.

Glorene pulled out her cigarette case and lit a cigarette before answering, clouding the air with blue smoke and taking away Kassie's appetite for the rest of her dessert. "Fond is a rather outdated word." Glorene paused. "You really are an old-fashioned girl. Perhaps because of being brought up by grandparents."

Kassie wanted to remind her that Glorene had been brought up by the same grandparents, but she refrained. "More than fond then?" she asked, returning to her original topic.

"Much more." Glorene thoughtfully sucked at her cigarette, then glanced at Kassie's half-eaten sherbet. "Does the smoke bother you?"

Surprised by this rare opportunity for honesty, Kassie nodded. "Yes, it does. A great deal."

Grinding out the cigarette in the glass ash tray, Glorene muttered, "Why didn't you say so before?"

"You never asked, and besides it's your home. Are you traveling to Florida alone?"

"Creighton thought that would be best. He's given me the contacts to make. They're expecting me. I don't really want to be away..."

"From your office?"

"From Creighton." She continued to push the long wrinkled cigarette round and round. "I hate to be away from him for even a minute."

"That bad, huh?"

"That bad. Crazy, isn't it? I'm usually so level headed. In all these years I've been divorced, I've been so busy building a business, I've not had time for men."

"I thought Mr. Hollister was married." After she'd said it, she wished she hadn't.

Glorene gave her a mildly pained expression. "What difference does that make in this day and age? Heavens, Kassie. Such a prude. Creighton's wife doesn't want him and never has. He's divorcing her as soon as the election is over. He's just biding his time."

Kassie ate another bite of the melting sherbet. "He loves you too?"

Glorene didn't look up. "Of course, silly. Very much." She was quiet a moment. "He's a wonderful man."

Kassie started to ask Glorene why Creighton wanted to see her tomorrow, but then she said instead, "What time are you leaving?"

"Early," Glorene answered absently. "About seven, I think. Guess I'd better pack."

"Want any help?"

"I've packed before, Kassie."

Kassie winced. "I'm sure you have. I just thought..."

"Sorry. I guess I'm on edge. It would be a greater help to me if you'd take care of the kitchen to such a degree that Leomia wouldn't get on my case."

"That I can do," Kassie promised and tried to give Glorene a reassuring smile. Her smile wasn't returned.

Glorene slowly rose, scooped up the sleeping Natty from the corner, and left the dining room.

Kassie had always loved puttering around the kitchen, but understandably, Leomia wanted no one in her domain, so the opportunity was rare indeed. As she loaded the dishwasher and wiped off the countertops, she considered the dead-end street her sister was traveling down, working for a man she loved and waiting helplessly for him to be free of his marriage vows. Kassie didn't envy her a bit. She wished she could talk honestly with Glorene. But would she ever listen?

A new Glorene awakened the next morning. Kassie had set her alarm early to ensure she was on hand to say good-bye. She was in the kitchen asking Leomia about her sick grandchild, when Glorene strode in, tall and regal in a trim plaid suit. The aura of success swirled thickly about her as though she'd never stepped out of it the night before. Quickly and with little conversation, she finished off two of Leomia's airy biscuits and a cup of coffee, then brought out her bags and called a cab.

"Isn't Creighton taking you to the airport?" Kassie was surprised.

"His time is valuable now," Glorene explained. "I insisted that he not."

Kassie didn't say anything more. But in the back of her mind, she thought of her appointment to meet with him at nine. If his time were that valuable, why would he want to see her? And why would Glorene take a cab, while Loren was ordered to come pick up Kassie? Somehow, Mr. Hollister didn't seem like a man deeply in love with her sister.

As Glorene went out the front door, Kassie shook her head. Everything was up to par for life in Westport—as usual, nothing made any sense.

eight

Loren was precisely on time. "I'll get it," Kassie called out when the chimes sounded. She swallowed back her quickening of excitement at seeing him again. Opening the door, she was taken once again with the soft clear blue of his eyes. He was dressed casually, and she immediately felt overdressed in the blush-pink silk dress. But how was she to know what to wear when she had no idea of the nature of her appointment?

"Greetings." His face wore its usual serious expression.

"You're on time." She shot him a teasing grin. "Come on in. I'm nearly ready. You've met Leomia?"

Leomia was peering suspiciously across the massive front room from the kitchen door.

"I've seen her from a distance when I was here before."

"This is Loren Marcellus, Leomia. A friend of Creighton's."

Only at this last statement did Leomia relax. "A friend of Creighton's? Well, all right. Hello, Mr. Marcellus." She strode across the room. "Yes," she said upon closer inspection. "I remember you now. Where're you two off to?"

"Leomia, really," Kassie chided her. "You're as bad as Glorene."

"Don't worry," Loren assured her. "I'm just taking her to see Creighton."

"Creighton?" Leomia's voice raised a pitch. "Whatever for?"

"We're not sure what Creighton wants." Kassie looked up at Loren. "At least I *assume* we don't know what Creighton wants. I for one don't know."

Loren shrugged to prove his innocence in the matter. "No one tells me anything. I'm the gopher, and today's orders were to gopher Kassie Carver and bring her to campaign headquarters."

Headquarters? Kassie had envisioned meeting Creighton at his downtown office, not in the political setting. Perhaps she shouldn't have been so quick to agree to all of this.

But Loren's glance at his watch hastened her to her room to grab her purse before Leomia could further embarrass her. Never had she had so many keepers. How had she managed to run the Double-C Ranch almost single-handedly before it had sold?

"Don't worry about supper, Leomia," Kassie said as they were leaving. "I'll just grab a sandwich. No sense cooking for just one."

"That's fine, honey. I'll see to it there are cold cuts in the refrigerator." With a stern look at Loren, she quipped, "Mind your manners, young man."

"Oh, yes, ma'am. I sure will," Loren replied, then chuckled deep in his throat as he closed the apartment door. "Charming lady," he said.

Kassie was glad to hear him laugh. "Leomia's smart, devoted, and very determined," she said. "I'm sure *charming* must be there on the list as well."

Sean's racy little coupe had not surprised her, but Loren's older model Mustang did. Unthinking, she had assumed he would flaunt his wealth the same as Sean had. She should have known better.

He must have caught her expression as he opened the

car door. "It runs," he said simply. "Keeps me from getting sold on my glorified heritage."

"It beats mine. I sold a battered old Ford pickup in Wyoming before I moved here." It made her uncomfortable that he felt he had to explain.

Loren was silent as he drove out onto the inter-dispersal loop and headed across town in a direction Kassie had not yet traveled.

"You're a law student?" Kassie cut the silence with a stab at conversation."

He nodded. "Uh huh."

"And Roger was a law student as well?"

"Uh huh again."

"Nice you were both interested in the same things."

"I'm a business administration major. Graduated two years ago."

"When did you decide to study law?"

"When Roger died."

"Not before?"

"Nope."

She was silent a moment, reaching to grasp the full meaning of what he was saying.

"Roger had high ideals," he said, which didn't explain much.

"You're going to try to live them out for him?"

"I guess you could say that."

"Are you sure he would have wanted you to?"

Loren didn't answer.

The Broadmore shopping mall was one of the largest in the region, and when they drove in the parking lot, no one could have missed that the Hollister campaign headquarters was located in the midst of it. One of the storefronts with an outside entrance sported patriotic streamers, banners, and bunting, which fluttered about the windows and the doorway.

"Wild, isn't it?" Loren parked the car, but made no move to get out.

"Quite," she agreed, surveying the panorama of posters sporting Creighton's likeness. "How unnerving to meet your own photo in such large dimensions every day."

"Only politicians and their ilk can handle it," he said. "They become quite addicted to having glorified opinions of themselves."

"Will it be the same for Creighton?"

Loren gave a half-smile. "Who knows? Everyone responds to success and power in a different way."

"I thought they all responded the same—by giving in to all the pressures."

"Some have been known to survive intact," he said. "A miracle, of course. But some do."

"Perhaps Creighton will."

"Perhaps he'll lose the election."

Funny, Kassie hadn't thought about that. But after all, he was in opposition to a powerful incumbent who had many loyal and, no doubt, well-paid workers who cared little about how violent the race became. Nor how dirty. "He may lose," she agreed thoughtfully, "but he's fighting hard, isn't he?"

"You gotta give the guy credit. He's a nice guy in a rough game. I just hope he doesn't get hurt." For a moment Loren looked at her as though he were going to say something else, but then he caught himself and thought better of it. "We'd better get in there. I don't want to make you late for your appointment."

He assisted her from the car and steered her toward the circus of color before them. Loren pushed open the door of headquarters and let her enter first.

The place was noisier and busier than Kassie had ever imagined. Rows of phones jangled incessantly, a few of which were being answered by volunteers who were on the job early. Several computer consoles were also manned by faithful volunteers. Other volunteers were stuffing envelopes at a far table.

Creighton was leaning against the edge of a table with a phone tucked between his ear and his shoulder, riffling through a stack of papers in his hands. He looked every inch the polished politician in a custom tailored iron-gray suit which complemented his silvery hair. He gave them a warm smile of greeting and, with the sheaf of papers, waved them toward a makeshift office in the back.

Loren led her through the noise and confusion, offering her a chair in the sparsely furnished office. "This is where I leave you. Coffee before I go?"

"Leave? Where to?" She knew the bereft feeling that washed over her was childish, but she'd assumed he would stay close. She hardly knew Creighton Hollister, and all this secrecy was terribly unfair.

"Other errands. I'm the gopher, remember?" He laid his hand on her shoulder. "I'll be back to take you home. Cream?"

"And sugar."

In a moment, he handed her the steaming styrofoam cup, milky with cream, a skinny stir rod sticking from it. At the same moment, Creighton made his entrance. He shook her hand warmly, almost causing her to spill the coffee.

"Kassie Carver! Here you are. How kind of you to come to this clamorous place to see me. Thank you. I had several appointments here today and there was no way I could have met you elsewhere." Creighton closed the door.

"Now, young lady, let's get down to business. As you may know, I'm planning to re-open Blackburn Stables soon and make the place come alive. You've seen the place, haven't you? Oh yes, you were with us that day, weren't you—when we first met Loren. Wonderful guy, isn't he?"

He paused and she politely inserted a "Yes, sir." For all that his words were smoothly brisk, she saw a warmth in Creighton's eyes when he spoke, and she heard caring in the tone of his voice. Kassie could understand why Glorene had fallen hopelessly in love with him. Still, she wondered if the feeling were truly mutual, as Glorene had claimed. Somehow, she sensed that Creighton's feelings for her sister were very different from hers for him; Kassie even suspected that Creighton had no idea he had made a fissure in Glorene's armor against men.

"The riding club, we have decided, will remain under Mr. Blackburn's management for a time. He has a great way not only with horses, but with the guys who work with them."

The phone buzzed. "Please excuse me. When you have volunteers rather than a trained secretary, they don't always hold calls as they've been asked." Briefly, he took care of the call and then returned his attention to her.

"Mr. Blackburn's failures," he continued, "were in promotion, or the lack of it. And in financial matters. His books were a disaster. I have an accountant out there now taking care of picking up the pieces and putting them together again."

Kassie was having difficulty concentrating on what he was saying about the stables. She was thinking instead about Glorene traveling alone to Florida this morning. What would her sister be doing in this office had she been here? Possibly she would have been in charge of preventing interruptions for Creighton. Glorene, who had several secretaries of her own in her office. What an ironic twist.

"It looks like we could be ready to re-open in a couple of weeks if all goes well. And if I'm able to get the right people for the right positions. That, my dear Kassie, is why I wanted to talk to you."

Suddenly Kassie was jolted from her thoughts. "Me?"

"Kassie, I'd like you to take over the office at Blackburn Stables. Straighten up the file system, contact previous customers, set up class schedules, and do the billing. Office management, yes. But more. I see it as a multi-faceted job position, in which you may at times be asked to serve as a hostess."

Kassie's heart was thumping wildly. "You're offering me a job at the stables?"

"Precisely. You'll be perfect for it, because of your combined knowledge of horses and your secretarial skills. You may have a little trouble with Mr. Blackburn at first. He's been used to running it as his own business. I'm taking a risk in letting him stay. But he's so adept at what he's doing, I can't afford to let him go at this point."

She leaned back and took a sip of the hot coffee. "Did Glorene ask you to do this?"

Creighton smiled. "Not at all. She merely planted the idea in my mind the evening we were at the Rhapsody. She's said nothing further, except to mention that the Quillian job fell through. I can assure you, Kassie, she's been too busy with real estate and an election campaign to pay attention to a riding club. Although I understand your asking."

The swivel chair squeaked as he turned toward her.

"While I highly respect Glorene's abilities, I've sensed that she underestimates your talents and your independent nature."

"It's that obvious?"

"I believe it's the new experience of being responsible for someone other than herself. You're a bit of a threat to her, Kassie, and for that reason, she's struggling to keep an upper hand."

"Me, a threat?"

"Anyway," he waved off the subject, "I know for a fact that she's very fond of you."

"As she is also of you, sir," she added quickly.

"I appreciate her sharp business mind," he said. "She's an extraordinary person."

But what about love? Kassie wondered. If Creighton did not love Glorene, was her sister headed for a crash? Compassion rose up in Kassie for her sister who had so adeptly wrapped herself in money, possessions, and success. Surely someday Kassie could ask Creighton to be honest with Glorene—to tell her he didn't love her.

"The other thing I'm asking you to do," Creighton said, leaving the subject of Glorene behind, "is to develop promotional ideas. No business, however good the product or service, will ever succeed without proper promotion. The name must appear before the public often."

He leaned back. "As you know," he swept his hand toward the outer office, "I'm very busy these days. So you can filter your ideas through Loren to me. He'll have a hand in the stable operations as well. I value his opinions and his ability to work as a liaison between Mr. Blackburn and me." Creighton reached for his briefcase, placed it on the desk, and flipped the locks open. "The first project we've planned is an overnight trail ride down around

Weller's Coves. Ever been there?"

She shook her head. "Was that Loren's idea?" she asked.

Creighton shuffled through the papers in the case and finally pulled out what he was looking for. "Mm. I believe it was. Original, isn't it? This will be a family-type outing. Bound to bring back some of the former clients of the stables. Here's a map of the area."

He handed the map to her across the desk. She could recognize little on the map except for the many inlets.

"This will be one of the times when you will serve as a good-will ambassador and hostess. How does that sound? Do you accept my offer?"

"Back in the saddle, and being paid for it." Kassie gave a merry little laugh. "It sounds too good to be true." Surely this was why she had felt the reluctance to sign on with the Quillian's that very first day. "When do I begin?"

"I want you there twice a week until we open." Pausing a moment, he said, "Excuse me a moment while I see if Loren is back."

He stepped to the door and called Loren's name above the raucous noise. A dozen or more volunteers must have arrived just since they'd been talking.

Loren's tall frame filled the small office as he entered. Kassie caught the spicy fragrance of his cologne, triggering the memory of his kiss outside Glorene's apartment. Involuntarily, she shivered.

"Is it time to take her home?" he asked.

"Not just yet. How's your schedule for the day, Loren?"

"Free day, sir. I was going to stick around here and see what needed to be done."

"How about you, Kassie?"

"I left the day open, not knowing how long this would take."

"Good." Creighton stood and slapped the desk top with his hands. "Both of you are on salary for the day then. Loren, take her to Blackburn's and let her spend a couple of hours looking over the office. Tend to Blackburn and make sure he doesn't give her any trouble. Do what few things you can around there to give me some idea of where to go from here—both of you. I need advice. Expert advice."

"Anything else?" Loren asked.

"That's it, kids. Go for it. And thanks," he added.

The car was quite warm when they came out. Loren fiddled with the controls to get the air conditioning going. "It doesn't work too good," he apologized.

"Hey, I'm so excited, I wouldn't even notice."

"Excited?"

"About my new job at Blackburn's."

"Creighton asked you to work full time?"

Her mind was already in a whirl of how she would go about fixing up the office. "Yes, full time. Can you believe it? Isn't it wonderful?"

Loren watched carefully for traffic as he eased out of the mall parking lot onto the busy highway. "I had a hunch that's what it might be, but since I wasn't sure, I didn't say."

"This is exactly what I've been praying for. The right job for me. God promised He'd give abundantly above what I could ask or even think of. And He certainly did it this time. I would have never thought of being able to work around horses in a city like Westport!"

Loren glanced over at her. "You sound like Roger again. Every time he got wound up about something he'd spout Scripture."

"It's the joy of the Lord," she said. "I always know He's

with me, but then there are times like this when He pours out the blessings. I get so excited!"

"Just because you got a job? And what if the job bottoms out? Will you still say God is doing more than you can think to ask?"

Kassie thought a moment. "I try not to play what-if games in the negative. When bad things happen, such as a job not turning out right, He's still given me His word that He will see me through everything in life—good or bad. No matter what."

"No matter what?" Loren asked.

"No matter what."

"I'm going to stop at the house for a few minutes before we go out to Blackburn's," he said, changing the subject. "Do you mind?"

"Not at all. Although I'll have to admit, I'm eager to get my hands into those files."

"You'll change your mind when you see what a mess they're in. The whole office has been a disaster area ever since I've been there. But don't worry, this won't take long."

Kassie had assumed he meant his apartment, and was totally unprepared as he drove into one of Westport's more affluent neighborhoods with gently curving tree-lined streets and sprawling homes set back from the street.

The Marcellus Mansion, as she'd heard Creighton call it, was banked by sweeping manicured lawns, edged by precisely clipped shrubbery and weedless flower beds coming into bloom. The rosy brick three-story house was fronted by a tiered white portico. The glossy-leafed magnolias, and sweet gum and beech trees dappled the carpet of grass with splotches of shade in the warm sunshine.

"This is lovely," Kassie said, craning around to take it

all in. "Did you grow up here?"

Loren gave a dry laugh. "Lived here all my life. We're thinking of having it made into a museum. Perhaps they'll make a waxen image of Dad and place it in the front hall. Coming in? There's still no fee at this point. Can't guarantee that forever."

"Yes, I'd like to see the inside."

She stepped out as he opened the car door, then followed him up the broad steps to the entryway.

"We haven't time for a full tour today." His voice echoed slightly in the vast marbled hallway. "Wait here. I'll be right back. Some of my riding gear is still here, which I've been meaning to pick up."

He waved her to a velvet-tufted antique chair against the wall. She opted to look about instead at the art work hanging in the hallway. She watched Loren go up the winding staircase two steps at a time. Briefly, she imagined him and Roger as little boys, sliding down the polished banisters, shrieking with giggles as they went.

Kassie was stepping around an urn on a pedestal to inspect a portrait in pastels when she was startled by a harsh, raspy voice.

"Well, well, now," the voice boomed at her. "Kassie Carver—the girl from way out west."

Kassie whirled around with a gasp, but she saw no one.

"Here. I'm in here."

Taking a few steps, she found herself looking into a library lined with floor-to-ceiling shelves of books. Seated in his wheel chair before a table set with a checker game was Vaughn Marcellus. The chair on the opposite side of the game table was empty. He waved her to it. "Sit down," he ordered in the same brash manner he'd displayed at the Rhapsody Club.

Part of her wanted to run out the front door, but the other part of her was frozen looking at him, locked by his icy gaze. "Have you no ears, child? Come in and sit down. I'm quite harmless and I've never been known to bite."

Stiffly, she moved toward the empty chair and sat down. The room had a musty smell, as though it was closed off a great deal.

"Do you play?"[1] he asked.

"Some." Surveying the board, she could see it was a tight battle and wondered if he had actually played alone up to this point.

"Be my guest." He gestured for her to join in.

Slowly at first, she entered into his game, then more swiftly as she saw openings appear. She was sure he had planted the openings as traps, and yet she slid into them. She had played countless checker games with Grandpa, but Grandpa had had no use for traps. He simply played to win.

The battle was heated for a time until at last Attorney Marcellus had but three kings left, then, with calculated and merciless precision, he began to pick off her men until she was down to one pitifully trapped king.

"Looks as though you've been beaten, young lady."

"Yes," she agreed, rubbing sweaty palms together, "so it does."

"Looked easy for a time, didn't it? Deceptive as life itself, a checker game." Mr. Marcellus focused his cold stare upon her. "I understand you're a very religious person, Miss Carver."

Kassie straightened in her chair. "I'm a Christian, if that's what you mean. It's a relationship..."

"Regardless of the glossy semantics, it's all the same. It was the downfall of my son Roger. The greatest detriment to his becoming all that he could have become."

"But I thought..."

"That Roger was killed in a plane crash? He was. But he was dead before that to me. Barraging me constantly with that wretched, mush-mouth religious talk." The large man turned the wheel chair abruptly and wheeled to the nearby window.

Kassie glanced about the room to the stone mantel above the fireplace. There hung portraits of two handsome young men. One was unmistakably Loren, the other had to be Roger. Looking at the slender face, set with eyes almost as lovely as Loren's, she wished she could have known him. She had an idea she and Roger would have gotten along famously.

After a moment, Vaughn moved slowly back to the table. "From all outward appearances, Loren and I look to be miles apart." His voice was steady, void of emotion. "Don't be deceived as you were in this simple game, child. Loren is now, and always will be, in my court and on my team. Although he is loathe to admit it just now, he and I are profoundly alike. Profoundly alike." His wide hands gripped the arms of the chair, turning the skin white and accentuating the growth of dark hair across the backs of his hands. "Your religion, or whatever you call it, has a wilting effect, Miss Carver. A hideous softening effect that I can't afford to have polluting my son's mind."

"Mr. Marcellus!" Suddenly she was impatient with this hardened man. "Loren and I..."

"Don't interrupt!" The voice was biting. "Whether you like it or not, you are in a precarious position because of your sister's strong political affiliations here in Westport. For her sake, and for yours, I suggest you listen and we'll have no problems, you and I."

"Loren and I happen to have the same employer," Kassie broke in. She had no way of knowing how much he knew, or how much Loren wanted him to know. "It looks as though we will be in one another's company a great deal in the future."

Vaughn tapped his fingertips together thoughtfully. "Ah. I see you're a very determined woman, Miss Carver. Let me put it this way. Be in his company as much as you like, but keep your religious garbage to yourself."

Straining, Vaughn Marcellus pushed himself higher in the chair and leaned forward slightly. "I *won't* have Loren's mind ruined by your Christian rubbish. I lost one son to it, and I am determined I will not lose the other. The cost to me is immaterial. Whether it involves harm to you, your sister, or your new employer—the candidate for mayor of Westport. Do I make myself clear?"

Fear, clutching her insides, nearly closed her throat. "Perfectly clear, Mr. Marcellus," she said in a whisper.

How could this man know so much about her life? Kassie was relieved to finally hear Loren's firm footsteps echoing in the front hall as he descended the stairs. "Kassie?" he called.

nine

"Did he win?" Loren asked as they drove slowly out of the circular drive and back onto the street.

"Win?"

"The checker game. He's a heartless player. Or didn't you notice?"

"I noticed. And yes, he won." Vaughn's cruel threats were still ringing in her ears. How dare he attempt to manipulate her life as well as Loren's? "He coerced me into several plays and then came in for the kill."

"Sounds sickeningly familiar. When I was little, he would challenge me to play and let me think I was winning, then swoop in at the last minute and wipe the board clean." Loren was quiet a moment. "I still don't know why it devastated me so. But every time, I ran to my room and cried. Maybe it was because he laughed when I lost."

Kassie pictured the little boy Loren, crushed and wounded by his own father, and the image made her heart break. "Then it wasn't the plane crash that made him this way? He was bitter before?"

"It's difficult for a kid to evaluate a parent, especially when that kid is so desperately looking for comfort and acceptance. But as I look back, I see that my father always had a sinister nature. The accident only made him worse."

"And your mother. How has this affected her?"

"She's withdrawn into a self-imposed shell." His voice

98

was low and intense. "The loss of Roger nearly devastated her. I'm sure deep down she blames Dad, but I've never heard her say it. Still, she feels it's her duty to stand by him. Saving face in the community is more like it."

"Perhaps she still loves him," Kassie said.

"Could be," Loren answered her, "but I seriously doubt it."

Kassie was relieved to enter the cool interior of the stables, breathing in the pungent hay and leather aromas she loved so well. Mr. Blackburn greeted them cordially and was not as reluctant to work with them as Creighton had suggested he might be. Kassie was introduced to the newly-hired stable hands, Travis Williams, a lanky blond-haired youth, and Joe Hopkins, better known as Wooster. Kassie immediately liked the grinning, friendly teen boys who shared her innate love of horses.

The office was dusty and cluttered. A fair amount of cleaning and scrubbing was required before she could begin any other jobs. Cleaning supplies were easily located in a storage closet. Even an old shirt was there that she could put over her clothes like a smock. As the dust and dirt were flying, the boys teased her about obliterating the stable atmosphere by her cleaning binge.

Loren passed by the door just then and added, "Before you know it, she'll have curtains at the windows and mats at the door. We'll have to wipe our boots before entering."

"Or take the boots clear off," Wooster added with a high-pitched giggle.

She joined in the bantering. She loved to see Loren's soft eyes sparkle with laughter. Perhaps this opportunity would be good for him—the chance to work at something that was removed from family contacts.

Kassie rummaged through the files and found long lists of former patrons who could be re-contacted as the opening date approached. By mid-afternoon she stopped work to stroll out of the office into the stable area.

Loren was giving Jolly Roger another workout in the arena. When he was on that horse a different expression clouded his face. He seemed to find little pleasure in the activity.

Travis and Wooster interpreted her appearance as a sign for them to take a break.

"Want a Coke?" Travis asked her, heading for the vending machines.

"Sure."

"You got it," he called back.

As the boys walked back from the machines, Wooster tossed the chilled can to her. Instantly, her reflexes responded and she caught it with ease.

Wooster's face lit up with appreciation. "Good catch. You learn that on the ranch?"

She shook her head as she opened the tab top. "Girls' softball team. Three years."

Together they leaned against the railing and watched Loren. "Man, he's a whiz on those jumps, isn't he?" Wooster said. "Why's he working so hard? Every time I see him he's practicing."

"He said he's competing in some big horse show," Kassie answered, letting the drink wash the dust from her throat. "I forget the name. The Royal-something or other. Royalite?"

Travis looked surprised. "The Royaliste? Hey, that's stiff competition. The toughest there is. People come from all over the country to enter. No wonder he's knocking himself out. But he sure doesn't need the dough." He shook his head. "Seems sort of crazy."

Kassie watched Loren again. Horse and man were united as one unit as they met and conquered each jump with grace and agility. What *was* the motivation behind the endless hours of work? Was it pressure from his father? Or was he doing it for Roger, the same way he was attending law school because of Roger? When, she wondered, would Loren Marcellus ever begin to live a life of his own?

Kassie fully intended to take the bus home, but Loren came in just before time for her to leave and said he would be taking her.

"Oh, no," she protested. "It's too far out of your way."

Her sense of being flattered quickly dissipated as he explained that Creighton had asked him to return her home. She shouldn't have cared one way or the other, but she felt a twinge of disappointment.

Thinking back to the warning from Vaughn, she almost laughed. Funny that he should think anything she said or did could ever influence Loren.

"Tell me about the Royaliste Horse Show," she asked him as they drove toward the city.

"What's there to tell? It's just a horse show."

"Just a horse show? Travis said it has the stiffest competition. I was curious why you chose it."

Loren ran his fingers through his hair, as always, curlier after being sweat-soaked beneath the rider's helmet. "Two years ago, Roger bagged the reserve championship in the Jumper Classic. He was going after the top prize when he died. I'm going to get it for him. It's as simple as that."

"What if you don't make it?"

He shot her a look. "That doesn't even enter my thinking."

"Seems rather stringent."

"Haven't you ever heard of someone picking up the cause of another and running with it?" A touch of irritation sounded in his voice.

She should have read his tone as a warning signal and let the subject drop, but she forged ahead. "I've heard of picking up another's cause because of a *belief* in the cause. That gives the person more of a heart for the battle—a heart to win."

"Are you suggesting that's not the case here?" The square jaws tightened.

"Only you can answer that."

"I thought I had, but obviously *you* have some doubts."

"A person with a heart to win is full of joy, even through the grueling preparation. When you're on Jolly Roger, there's no joy. You look like you're tied to the torture rack." She paused, picking words carefully. "I know enough about horse shows to know that even in lesser competitions, the overall manner of the rider counts a great deal."

"That's concentration you're seeing," he retorted. "It's taken time to teach Jolly Roger to trust me as much as he trusted Roger."

Kassie shifted in her seat and turned to gaze out the side window. "I'm sorry. I didn't mean to insinuate things. Forget I said anything."

But he wasn't ready to let it drop. "No, no," he said with a twinge of sarcasm. "Please explain yourself. I must know. How does one determine the difference between a heart to win and simply setting his mind to do something?"

Kassie wished she hadn't let her mouth get her into

this mess. "It's the calling of God," she told him. "When we search for God's perfect plan for our lives and delight in Him, He promised to give us the desires of our hearts. When it's God's calling, then we have the heart for it. When it's our own will that we're following, then we have only our own stubbornness to keep us going. It's like the difference between—between a dry stick and a live, growing tree."

Loren searched the block in front of Glorene's apartment for a parking space. When he found one, he whipped in quickly and came around and opened the door to help her out. "I don't believe in a calling from an impersonal God. All I've seen of God is harsh and judgmental. That's not for me. I'm going on gut-level feelings. And I *do* believe in Roger's quest for the Jumper Classic trophy."

"And his quest to be a fair attorney, right?"

"Yes!"

"But not his quest to faithfully serve his God?"

Loren's face paled. He stepped back suddenly as though she had struck him. "I'll call you when Creighton informs me of your next work day," he said stiffly. "Good-bye."

"Thank you for bringing me home," she called after him.

ten

Thankfully, Kassie was scheduled for work at the hospital that evening, giving her the opportunity to stay busy. She could push the incident with Loren out of her mind. How she wished she hadn't pushed him into a corner. She should have known he would be defensive.

As she changed into her uniform, she prayed for forgiveness for her brashness. She also asked for wisdom to say the right thing in future conversations. If there were any.

The pediatric ward had become her favorite place in the entire hospital. The last time she had been here, Mindy had greeted her by giving her names of children to pray for, and tonight was no different. Two girls were scheduled for surgery the next morning, and Mindy asked Kassie to lift them up to their heavenly Father.

"They're real scared, Kassie." Mindy sat cross-legged on her bed, looking up at Kassie with wide, innocent eyes. "If we ask God, He'll take the scaredness away, won't He?"

Kassie sat on the edge of the bed and took Mindy's hands. "The Bible tells us to ask, and we will receive," she said. As they prayed, Kassie marveled at the simplicity of the girl's faith. No wonder Jesus admonished Christians to come to Him as little children. How she wished that truth could be transmitted to Loren Marcellus.

Later, as she was reading horse stories aloud to the

children in the playroom, she told them about the Double-C Ranch and how she used to ride and round up cattle.

"Did you have spurs and chaps and everything?" one of the boys wanted to know.

"Everything," she said. "That's all part of the gear when you're doing ranch work."

"Can we see them?" he asked. "Do you still have them?"

"They're packed away and stored in Wyoming. A long way off."

The children gave groans of disappointment.

Kassie's mind was racing. "However, I could send for them." The children's fascination with horses and riding had given her a tremendous idea.

Later that evening in the cafeteria, she shared her idea with Holly over a cup of coffee. "What do you think about having a horse show for the children, held outdoors on the parking lot?" she asked. "The children who aren't able to come outside could watch from the windows. Could it work?" She explained her job at Blackburn's and her access to both horses and riders.

"We've had many programs to entertain the kids since I've worked here, but never a horse show." Holly's pixie face reflected her eager interest. "I think it's a marvelous idea. I can contact the officials and put through the request forms. But I'm sure we'd receive a go-ahead."

On napkins, they penned out notes of what such a program should include. By the time Kassie arrived back at the apartment the hour was fairly late, but she was wide awake, and because of the time difference in Wyoming, she could call Ted. He'd been kind enough to allow her to store many of her belongings in the attic of the ranch house.

Across the miles she detected a warmth and affection in Ted's voice. When she asked him to send the needed items, he said, "Don't tell me you've already found yourself an Eastern dude to ride with. That was mighty slick, Kassie."

Her mind flew to Loren. If Ted saw him, would he call him a dude? Briefly, she told him about the stables and her job there, then about the possible horse show for the hospital.

Ted promised to ship the gear to her right away. "I'll even put in a couple of your hats. Betcha you don't even have a good hat with you."

She snickered. "I don't think I would look too good walking around Westport with a cowboy hat on."

"That just proves them Easterners don't know nothing," he said slowly.

He shared the latest news about the ranch activities, then put the children on to talk to her. With much fuss and drama, Jessica and Joseph told her about the newest litter of kittens and what they were learning in school. Joseph knew exactly how many days were left until summer vacation.

Kassie was amazed at how much she missed them. She had thought of them very little in the past few weeks, but now their small faces came back to her along with the memory of how they'd clung to her the day she left.

"Onrushing Charger is going to foal," Jessica said in a grown-up voice.

"How exciting," Kassie said, fighting off the stabs of homesickness. "Give her a hug and a pat for me will you? And if it's a filly, I'll be back to buy her next year. Okay?"

"I'm gonna pray and pray that it's a filly," Jessica said,

"so you'll come back and see us."

As firmly as she could, Kassie told them all good-bye and hung up. But she could barely steer her thoughts back to Mindy and the kids at McKinley Memorial Hospital.

Funny thing, the subconscious mind, she thought as she peeled off her clothes and stepped into a steaming shower. *And a little tricky as well.* She had convinced herself that the ranch had been erased from her mind, but her longing for it had never left, only lurked in hiding just below the surface of her thoughts.

Later, clad in her gown and robe, with her wet hair swathed in a thick towel, she sat down at the dressing table to dry her hair. Suddenly, she realized that she was proceeding with plans for the horse show when she hadn't even cleared it with Creighton.

Hesitantly, she stepped to the phone to dial Loren. He'd given her the number of his apartment to keep in touch, and Creighton had instructed her to channel ideas through him. However, just as she was dialing the last number, the paunchy face of Vaughn Marcellus came before her, and she heard the echo of his cold, calculating threats.

She placed the phone back in its place. She would be wiser to talk to Loren during working hours than to make late night phone calls which could be misinterpreted.

With a tug, she pulled the towel from her head and shook out her hair. *This is stupid,* she thought as the dryer whined in her ear, succumbing to the fear of Vaughn's threats. Drawing a deep breath, she switched off the dryer, and punched the phone buttons.

"Come on, Loren," she whispered. "Please be there." But there was no answer. Nevertheless, she still felt a surge of victory as she hung up. To live in fear of that wicked man would be more destructive than anything he actually could do to her.

Her phone calls to Loren the next day were futile also. Finally, she phoned Creighton at campaign headquarters, apologizing for bothering him in the midst of all his busyness, and explained that she'd been unable to reach Loren.

"He's doing a little business for me today, Kassie," he said. "What's on your mind?"

Briefly, she shared with him her idea for the horse show at the hospital.

"Great idea, Kassie. Top notch publicity. You deserve a bonus for this one. We'll schedule it to coincide with our grand opening. I'll have Loren call you as soon as he gets back. He has something to tell you anyway."

Kassie couldn't imagine what Loren would have to tell her, but hearing the incessant phones ringing in the background, she didn't ask Creighton any more questions, except to quickly find out when Glorene was coming back into town. She jotted the flight number and arrival time on the note pad beside the phone.

When the phone rang later that evening, she rushed to catch it, assuming it was Loren. But a friendly male voice asked for Glorene.

"Glorene's out of town until Thursday. Is there something I can do?" she asked, disappointed it wasn't Loren.

"You sure don't sound like Leomia. Who am I speaking to?"

"This is Kassie Carver, Glorene's sister."

"Well, well. Little Kassie. You probably don't even remember me. This is Ben Paquette."

"Of course I remember you, Ben. It's been a long, long time. How are you?" In a rush, memories surged up from

Kassie's childhood of the charming, dark-eyed Ben who had melted the heart of a seventeen-year-old Glorene, then had eloped with her. Kassie had never known why they had divorced.

"I'm lonely, as usual. I try calling Glorene periodically to touch base to see where I stand. Do you know where she is?"

"Somewhere in Florida, I'm told."

"Florida?" He sounded elated. "Where?"

"I'm sorry, I don't know. She's there to observe the campaign of some mayoral race."

"Oh, yeah. I'd heard she's immersed in politics now. Who knows what'll come next."

They shared a few more amenities before saying goodbye. Kassie stood studying the phone. Glorene had never mentioned her ex-husband, and Kassie had assumed the split-up had been devastating. But Ben sounded quite friendly. *Strange.*

Loren's call came Wednesday night after she'd returned home from the hospital. "Catch the bus to the stables in the morning, Kassie," he told her. "Creighton wants you to work a few hours and I've got something to show you. A little surprise." His voice was kind, as though he'd forgotten the misunderstanding between them. She was relieved to know he could forgive and forget.

Her attempts at learning his secret were useless. "Don't press me," he said with a hint of a chuckle in his voice. "I've always been terrible about secrets. Just hurry out as early as you can."

ะ

Loren's lone car was parked in the lot beside the main building when she arrived the next morning, early as he had asked. Hurriedly, she made her way inside, uncertain whether she was excited about the surprise—or about seeing Loren Marcellus again.

The area lights were not on and the building was dim. Even the office was still dark. She needed a few minutes for her eyes to adjust to the blackness.

"Back here, Kassie," she heard him calling. "By Jolly Roger's stall."

Carefully, she made her way around the arena. Now she could make out his tall outline against the gray light from the high windows. He stepped toward her and reached out to take her hand, as full of excitement as a little boy. "Wait till you see," he said, pulling her along side his big strides.

He stopped at a stall, opened it, and made a sweeping bow. "Kassie Carver, meet Regalia's Interlude, or Regalia for short. Regalia, please meet Kassie."

There in the stall was the most regal sorrel filly Kassie had ever seen. Her name fit her perfectly. The clear white blaze on her nose was the only deviation from the deep, rich sorrel of her well-groomed coat. Her head was proud, but she had a gentleness in her eyes that Kassie sensed immediately. She was obviously well-bred and had been well cared for. "Oh, Loren," she whispered, as though a spoken word would break the spell. "She's so beautiful." She reached out to touch the silky nose and felt warm breath on her wrist. "Where did she come from?"

"I knew you'd like her. I picked her up in Roanoke yesterday."

Kassie ran her hand over the rippling shoulder muscles. "You're a lovely lady, Regalia, and rightly named."

Regalia replied with a soft nicker and nuzzled the sleeve

of Kassie's blouse. "She's much too wonderful to use here though. She shouldn't be just a trail horse for some greenhorn's riding lessons."

At that, Loren put his hands on her shoulders and turned her to face him. He seemed mildly embarrassed, but his smile was not the abbreviated one she usually saw. It was wide, warm, and wonderful, giving fuller light to the clear blue eyes. The dimples deepened. "I was so excited for you to see her, I didn't explain. She's yours, Kassie."

Her breath caught short. She searched Loren's eyes and found he wasn't kidding. "Why for me?"

He laughed at her look of disbelief. "Creighton's instructions were that you should have a special mount for the work here, and I was told to make the choice. He didn't want you to pick and grab from the other stock, so I made a special trip to Roanoke to get her for you. She's for your own personal use as long as you work here. And I'm sure he'd arrange an easy way for you to buy her later, if you fall in love with her. And it looks like you might."

The sharp awareness of Loren's hands holding her as he spoke was as powerful as the excitement surging through her at the thought of owning this magnificent horse.

"I knew exactly what I was looking for," he went on, his voice growing softer.

"You did?"

"Of course." His hand strayed from her shoulder to her collar, then under the thickness of her hair, where his fingertips caressed the softness of her neck. "For Kassie, a horse must be spirited, yet gentle. Strong and proud, yet not arrogant. Very much like Kassie herself..."

Her mind reeled as she looked deep into Loren's clear

blue eyes. His fingers were combing gently through the curls of her hair. The kiss he placed upon her waiting mouth was gentle and restrained. Her face lifted to meet it, and she yielded herself to his embrace.

Regalia's nickering seemed fuzzy and distant, as though it were in another place, another world. Or was she the one who had been transported into another world? Her heart was pounding in her throat, choking her breath into short little gasps. Loren was leaving a trail of soft kisses along her cheek down into the hollow of her neck as he drew her closer to him.

Somewhere in the distance, a pickup door slammed. That would be Harlis Blackburn coming to work. "You and Regalia need to get better acquainted," he whispered in her ear. "Let's go for our own ride this morning and I'll show you the trails. Mm?"

Kassie struggled to shake from her mind the fog that had clouded it. She pulled back from the hold of the muscular arms. "I *will* need to know the trails, won't I?"

He nodded, not willing to completely release her. His hand still clung to her arm. "And I'm your best teacher."

They heard the door slam at the side entrance by the office. Harlis hollered a loud "hello" and threw the switch that lit up the large overhead lights. Lights that surely must reveal every hidden emotion that was written on Kassie's face at that moment. Suddenly she felt ashamed. Ashamed that Loren's embrace had had such an impact upon her, when for him it was no doubt just another kiss— just another girl.

☙

Kassie developed an instant rapport with Regalia. The mount had received extremely fine training, and she handled with ease and agility. As they rode along the trails through the forests dripping dew, Kassie outlined to Loren her ideas about the horse show for the hospital. As Creighton had, Loren felt it was a good idea and seemed eager to assist.

At the edge of the trail, wild flowers displayed patches of pastels in the tangle of grasses among the thick trees. Surprised birds flew up ahead of them, scolding them for disturbing the peace of the spring morning. Cresting a hill, they came upon a shallow valley that cradled a small lake. The water breathed a foggy mist into the air, giving the scene a mystical aura.

Loren rode to the water's edge and dismounted, then helped her down. Neither spoke as they leisurely allowed the animals to drink their fill. The morning sun had topped the tree line and spilled into the placid waters, giving it a pink diamond effect.

"God's handiwork is amazing, isn't it?" Kassie said half to herself. She breathed deeply of the clean air.

Loren looked at her over Jolly Roger's back as he adjusted the cinch strap. "Is that all you ever think about—God?" His tone held no malice, yet the question was unsettling.

She thought a moment. "That's like asking if all a person thinks about is breathing." She tossed a pebble into the water and watched the ripples swell and grow to the edge of the water. "It's not so much a matter of thinking; it's a vital part of my being."

Loren came around Jolly Roger and stood beside her. "God is like that to you?"

"Yes, He is," she murmured not wanting to look up at him.

"How can that happen?"

"By knowing Jesus as Savior." How much could she say without offending him as before and wrecking the already delicate relationship? "Jesus said if we know Him, we know the Father."

"You make it sound so easy." He shook his head. "Like telling a person to put their brain to sleep."

"Not to sleep, Loren. But to take the intellect off the throne and let the Lord take full control. When God takes over, we can use our intellects to the fullest." She turned to pat Regalia and move her back from the water's edge to where the grass was thicker.

"It could never be that way for me." The gentleness had drained from his voice. "Too much has happened in my life." His voice cracked. "There's no room for naivete in the world of law and politics. Come on, we'd better get back."

Open his eyes, Lord, she prayed silently as she re-mounted Regalia. She knew she wouldn't be wise to utter another word.

After work that day, Loren drove her home, but the atmosphere was altered, as though he had never touched her. But he *had* touched her, she cried out in her mind. Selfishly, she clung to the memory of his arms around her, tender and controlled. And how had he told her he'd chosen Regalia just for her. Perhaps deep within Loren were feelings that even he didn't fully realize or understand. On the other hand, maybe she was the one lacking understanding—foolishly thinking the kiss meant something to him, as it had to her.

"Thanks for choosing Regalia for me," she said before stepping from the car. She had quickly insisted that he stay put and not open the door for her, for the late afternoon traffic downtown was horrendous. "You made the perfect choice. I love her."

"My pleasure," he replied. "I always appreciate having a fellow horse lover around."

&a

Later, as she showered and dressed to go meet Glorene's plane, she mulled over the trite term, "fellow horse lover." Was that all she was to him?

Since Glorene's car was at the airport, Kassie had decided to splurge and take a cab and surprise her sister. Glorene seemed both pleased and disgruntled when she saw Kassie waiting at the ramp for her. Weariness circled the captivating green eyes.

"So you talked to Ben, did you?" Glorene asked in a tight voice as they unlocked her trunk and loaded the suitcases. "Did you have to tell him where I was?"

"I didn't. I didn't even know. I just told him it was somewhere in Florida. Want me to drive?" Glorene looked so tired. Glorene shot her a reprimanding look. "I can drive, Kassie." She walked around to the driver's side and let herself in. "Florida was one word too many for Ben," she said as they pulled out of the parking lot. "He lives there. He's like a bloodhound. He found me."

"Is that bad?" Kassie wanted to know, thinking of the friendly voice on the line the evening she had talked with him.

Glorene sighed deeply as though the question were terribly redundant, then chose not to answer, her mouth remaining grim.

Kassie changed the subject and shared the latest news about the job at Blackburn's.

"Creighton hired *you*?" Glorene asked with open surprise. "Full time? Well, I'll be... Boy, you just never know, do you?"

"You were the one who first suggested it. At the club that night. Remember?" Kassie felt her exasperation rising. It would have served Glorene right if no one had met her silly plane.

"At the Rhapsody? When Loren was with us?" She gave an empty laugh accompanied by a shrug. "I only meant for you to help get things started. To lay groundwork. But a permanent position..."

Glorene didn't explain herself further and Kassie didn't press. Obviously, Glorene either didn't think she could handle such a position, or she was surprised to think Creighton would hire her. Whichever it was, Glorene's estimation of her sister was as low as usual. On a scale of one to ten, Kassie figured she rated about a one-and-a-half with Glorene. And the struggle against bitterness was becoming a constant battle.

When they were entering the door of the apartment, with Natty barking wildly at their feet, the thought hit Kassie. Now that she had a full time job, plus the bonuses Creighton promised, she would begin the search for an apartment of her own. The thought lifted her spirits, and partially made up for the lack of appreciation from her sister.

eleven

The excitement of the upcoming horse show had everyone at Blackburn's in a tizzy. Had they taken on too much, trying to do the show and plan for the grand opening on the same weekend? But Holly had cut through plenty of red tape to acquire permission from hospital officials, and the green light was flashing.

Kassie plunged into the task with a glad and thankful heart. The work was challenging but stimulating. And she was certainly more than ready to be faced with some challenging stimulation!

She contacted former customers, both by phone and letter, and found that many were pleased about the reopening. Details for the upcoming overnight family trail ride were being worked out by the staff as well.

The more Kassie did in the office, the more she found to do. Finally, she called Creighton to inquire if she could increase her hours. "Otherwise," she told him, "we'll never be ready for the grand opening."

Creighton agreed to the overtime. "By the way, Kassie, I could use a little of your expertise over here at campaign headquarters. Can you serve as a volunteer a couple evenings a week?"

"I don't know a thing about politics," she told him. "I'm afraid I wouldn't be much help."

"It takes all the little people like you and me working together to clean up a city from the likes of Jasper

Bosworth. My mother always used to say, 'Many hands make light work.' Your youth and enthusiasm are exactly what I need to help make this thing go. What do you say?"

She could not refuse, and she was surprised to find that she *wanted* to help Creighton. Although she didn't approve of Glorene's play for him, she had begun to surmise that Creighton wasn't really a party to it. "Anything I can do will have to be squeezed in between my job and my volunteer work at the hospital," she told him.

"Sounds like there might be an hour or so to spare," he remarked lightly. "Just call and let me know when you can come."

Kassie didn't protest any more. Still, she wasn't sure when she'd have time considering the myriad of details she was suddenly faced with at Blackburn's.

Sean phoned her at the apartment several times, asking to see her. At first, she was reluctant to see him, but when he continued to act like a gentleman and to treat her with utmost respect, she found she rather liked his company.

Evening concerts were underway at the Ronson Gardens, and together they enjoyed the music presented in the lovely open air amphitheater in the midst of the lush gardens. Sean further surprised her by accepting an invitation to attend church one Sunday.

He listened intently to the sermon, then asked Kassie to introduce him to the young pastor. As they were driving home, he commented, "He doesn't really act like what you'd think a pastor would. He seems like a regular guy to me."

Kassie laughed. "Most Christians I know are regular people, Sean."

On the afternoon before the horse show at McKinley Memorial, the children were filled with endless questions about the horses. Kassie had shown them her silver-studded bridle she'd won in barrel racing as a teenager. The children passed it around, touching the shiny silver and trying to figure out how it fit on a horse's head.

As Kassie was preparing to leave, Mindy was by her side, her little face upturned. "Are you going to visit the sad lady before you go home today?" she asked.

Kassie had talked to Mindy one day about Lexi. Without mentioning names, she simply asked Mindy to pray for a sad lady on the eighth floor, that she might get well soon. Since then, Mindy had become very interested in the "sad lady."

"I visit her every time I'm here, Mindy. Why?"

"I've been thinking about her a lot. Would you take her this?" She handed Kassie a small folded piece of paper.

Kassie studied the girl's serious face. "Of course. I'd be glad to." She wanted to explain to Mindy that her note might not do any good. Nothing at this point seemed to help Lexi who had her heart set on defeat rather than winning. The stubborn woman had simply lost the heart to win. But Kassie didn't want to say anything to discourage Mindy.

As usual, Lexi didn't want to talk, but Kassie read passages of Scripture anyway. She was determined to continue until Lexi told her to stop. But Lexi said nothing at all, merely lay there buried in the covers. Before leaving, Kassie placed the note from Mindy on the bedside table. As she did, she said, "Here's something on your table from a little girl in the pediatric ward who has leukemia."

Sharp words crackled from beneath the layers of covers. "So! You've been talking about me have you?"

"I only mentioned to her that I visit a lady on the eighth

floor who doesn't have much to be happy about. That's true, isn't it?" Kassie spoke in hushed tones so as not to break this thin thread of contact. But Lexi had no more to say.

"I'll see you the next time I come," Kassie said. She quickly slipped out and went home.

≈

Saturday morning dawned brilliant and warm. Kassie was up before dawn. She quickly dressed in her jeans and Western-style shirt with the pearl snaps. In the things that Ted had sent were several of her hats. The gold one matched her shirt perfectly. She felt so good being dressed in the kind of duds she'd worn most of her growing up life—jeans, western shirt, hat, and boots. She fastened the belt with the silver buckle and surveyed her reflection in the full-length mirror. She looked like her old self again. She felt almost human!

"It's an admirable thing you're doing, Kassie," Leomia told her at breakfast, her round face beaming. "Using your talents to bring joy to those little ones. I'm busting with pride for you."

Kassie thanked her good friend, but she had little time for talk. She intended to be at the hospital early—but she also planned to be out of the apartment before Glorene was up and asking questions.

By eight o'clock, Wooster and Travis were at the hospital parking lot unloading the horses from the trailers. Even Harlis had come along to help with the show. A broad smile etched new wrinkles in his weathered face. Loren had driven out to the stables before seven in order to handle Jolly Roger himself. He trusted no one else to load the gelding. Kassie saw him arrive in the second pickup.

The nurses, aides, and volunteers were bringing the ambulatory children out onto the lawn under the sprawling oaks where they had a clear view of the parking lot. The lot had been cleared and cordoned off.

Kassie watched Loren step down out of the pickup and begin looking for her in the crowd. She shivered even though the warm sun was penetrating her long-sleeved shirt. Purposely, she waited until he spotted her and watched intently as his face lit up. Was she reading too much into his expression? Was he actually glad to see her?

He called to her to come and help unload Regalia, who had been tacked up by the boys.

"A real live cowgirl," Loren remarked as he looked her over. "And a dapper English squire," she countered with a smile, realizing their background differences were not a threat anymore.

She led the docile Regalia through the crowd of chattering children, letting them pet her velvet nose and reach up to feel the stiff ears. They giggled gleefully at the touch.

Mindy was busy helping with the younger children. Kassie marveled at how she was always reaching out to others—so mature for her young age.

Before the event began, Kassie took a moment to introduce Loren to Mindy. "I've heard a lot about you," he said, giving her a smile that was unrestrained.

"From Kassie?"

"Yes, from Kassie."

"Then it must have been good." Mindy smiled. "Kassie is my friend."

Loren knelt down by Mindy's chair, his bronze arms and hands a contrast against the child's pale skin. "It was all good," he assured her. "But now that I've met you, I know it was all true!"

Mindy warmed to the compliment, and gazed at Loren with worshipful eyes. "Thanks, Mr. Marcellus. And thank you so much for coming. All the children are excited."

"So are we, Mindy." Loren stood up and looked at Kassie with questions in his eyes that she could not decipher, then left to prepare for the show.

Kassie's performance wasn't as flamboyant as Travis' and Wooster's bareback riding stunts, nor as professional as Loren's breathtaking jumps. Had she been astride Onrushing Charger, she could have done a number of tricks. But the object here wasn't the performance but the audience contact. The excited cheers of the children gave proof of the show's success.

Harlis Blackburn himself stole the show. He rode his faithful old quarter horse around the lot, deftly looping his lasso over the heads of Travis and Wooster as they stood in the center. The children whooped and whistled and cheered.

They must have practiced secretly, because Kassie had never even seen Harlis on his horse. She was pleased they cared enough to give this extra effort.

When Loren was taking Jolly Roger flawlessly over the jumps, Holly came quietly to Kassie's side. "Don't look now," she whispered, "but we have another viewer—up on eighth."

Kassie's heart quickened. "Lexi?" She dared not look up.

"It's Lexi all right." Holly gave a rippling little laugh. "And to think she had to open those drapes to watch."

"Holly," Kassie said, "this could be the first step in her journey back to reality."

Later, as Loren, Harlis, and the boys loaded the mounts back into the trailers, Kassie assisted in taking the children back to their rooms. As she did, Mindy called her aside and showed her a note. On it was penned one word: "Maybe."

"What's this?" Kassie turned the paper over in her hands.

"It's my answer from the sad lady. I invited her to watch the show from her window," Mindy said. "Anyhow, she answered me. That's a good sign, isn't it?" Her eyes were wide with questioning.

"She did more than answer." Kassie put her arm around Mindy's shoulders. "Holly saw her at the window. The window that's had the curtains closed for weeks."

Mindy clapped her thin hands. "Oh, wow! Neat! Now maybe she won't be so sad."

"We'll all keep praying," Kassie told her.

On the way back to the stables, Kassie rode between Harlis and Loren, with Loren at the wheel. With youthful exuberance, Travis and Wooster sped on ahead in the other pickup.

Kassie mulled over the miracle of Lexi and longed to share the terrific news, but she was careful to heed the doctor's warning not to speak of Lexi to anyone. But her excitement was near the exploding point.

"Sure don't take much to get you happy, little lady," Harlis commented in his gravelly voice. "Ain't she pretty when she's happy, Loren?"

Loren took his eyes from the street traffic a moment to look at her. "She sure is, Harlis," he agreed lightly. "She sure is."

Loren's voice wrapped around her and drew her into its deep warmth. Suddenly, she felt overly warm and was thankful they had arrived at the stables, and she was able to step from the closeness of the pickup.

The five of them worked quickly to groom the horses and put the tack away. Wooster and Travis ended up in a grand water fight. But rather than get miffed with them as he usually did, old Harlis joined right in with the fun and laughter. The glorious morning had worked its spell on each of them.

The festivities of the grand opening in the afternoon provided a perfect follow up to the show that morning. Kassie was kept busy pouring cups of coffee and punch, handing balloons to the kids, and answering endless questions about the stable facilities. Several families and individuals signed up for the trail ride at Weller's Cove. Kassie found herself hoping the group would remain small enough for the staff to handle easily.

She was outlining the children's riding class schedules to a group of young mothers when she looked up and saw Sean smiling at her. Out of the corner of her eye she noticed him ambling about, waiting for her to be free. When he saw the opportunity, he hurried over to her.

"You look great, Kassie," he said, taking a lingering look at her Western garb. "Much as I hate to admit it— much as I wanted you in my own office—I can see this is where you really belong."

Kassie smiled. "You can see it now, but the Lord knew all along."

He reached out to take her hand. "It seems to work that way for you."

"It can work that way for *anyone*, Sean." She pulled her hand away.

"Hey," he said, spying the clipboard for the trail ride, "what's this?"

"An overnight trail ride for new clients. At Weller's Cove."

"Weller's Cove?" His eyes softened. "You'll be there?"

"I have to be. I'm the hostess for the event."

"What does it take to go?"

Reluctantly, she pushed the clipboard toward him. "Sign the sheet and pay the fee." In spite of the fact that she was coming to enjoy Sean's company, the trail ride was one place where she did not want his presence. With mixed emotions, she watched him sign the page on the clipboard.

&

The story of the hospital show and the grand opening made page two of the *Westport Gazette-Times*, complete with clear photos of the excited kids on the hospital grounds. The reporter did a good job of getting the names and facts straight. Creighton was pleased with all their hard work—and the publicity.

Kassie easily settled into the routine of working full time at the stables, and splitting her evenings and weekends between hospital work and helping at campaign headquarters. The basic function of a campaign, she soon learned, was plain old hard work. Phoning constituents, mailing hundreds of letters, and knocking on doors.

Creighton gave detailed plans outlining his stand on city's policies, which she studied carefully. She was not so naive as to think he could bring them all to pass if he were elected, but she admired his courage to stand for issues which were in direct opposition to Mayor Bosworth's policies in the past.

Several times, she and Loren were thrown together on trips "into the masses," as Creighton called them. Kassie handed out literature while Loren spoke to dock workers, housewives, and corporation executives with equal ease. He seemed to fit in wherever he was, and people listened. Kassie watched as he wisely handled hecklers who obviously had been set up by the opposition.

Amidst their busy schedules, Kassie and Glorene seldom saw one another. One evening, during a rare dinner together, Kassie asked Glorene if Creighton had a chance of winning.

Glorene paused to refill her coffee cup before answering. In the background, Leomia banged pots and pans around in the kitchen. "At first," Glorene answered thoughtfully, "I would have said no. He was such an unknown. Few people in Westport had ever heard of him. I told him he was crazy to run. I felt he was too good a person to be in politics. That Bosworth would eat him alive."

She twirled her spoon in the cooling coffee. "But we've been doing our homework, Baby. We've pulled scores of citizens into our camp. Once people see what a wonderful man Creighton is, they're on our side. It'll be a tight race, but our chances are improving daily."

She smiled. "Even Sean Phipps has been helping by creating our ads for a nominal fee." Glorene raised her neatly lined eyebrows. "By the way, thanks for paving the way for us to reach Sean. You did a better job than I ever thought you could."

Kassie was indignant. "I haven't spent time with Sean because of the campaign. As a matter of fact, if he hadn't made an effort to change his actions, I never would have seen him again."

Glorene gave a little snort of disbelief and waved it off. "Nevertheless, dear sister, you got Sean to do what we wanted and that's all that matters."

A few days later, Kassie rode the bus to Mom Tinsley's neighborhood, determined to locate her own place. If another apartment was available in the area, surely Mom Tinsley would know about it.

Kassie strolled up the walk to the wide front porch. A porch swing hung off to the side. The flowers that had been only a promise the first time she had come here were now a reality. The climbing roses were heavy with the tiniest of pink buds. She tapped at the door.

She was taken by surprise when the stooped little lady opened the door, then broke into a bright smile. "There you are! I knew the Lord would bring you back to me!"

Seeing Kassie's expression of astonishment, Mom Tinsley invited her inside and explained, "Just after you came to look at the place, another gal came along who had no mind at all to abide by the few rules I've given. She was out of here one day shy of a week." She shook her wizened little head. "So I just talked to the Lord and asked Him to send you back, and sure enough, He did."

Kassie laughed. *What a lady!* Over a cup of tea in Mom Tinsley's kitchen, Kassie wrote out the check for the deposit and acquired her new home. *Home!* What a lovely word, with a new intensity of meaning.

As Kassie rode the bus back into the city, she leaned back in the seat and watched the shaded boulevards passing by. She felt saturated with contentment and happiness. Happier than she'd been since she'd left Cody. In her heart, she praised the Lord for watching over her. She could hardly believe that Mom Tinsley had actually prayed to have her come back.

Her joy was short-lived, though. When she told Glorene of the upcoming move, her sister was more violently angry than she'd ever seen her.

twelve

"Move?" Glorene flared. "Away from here? Why you un-grateful child. Have you no concept of how hard it is to make it on your own? It costs a lot of money to live these days. You'll fall right on your face. If you had any sense at all, you'd stay right here where you have it easy." She lit a cigarette and the flicker from the lighter's flame cast shadows across her face.

"I'm not ungrateful," Kassie countered. "I've more than appreciated all you've done." Her mouth went dry and cottony as she searched for the right words. "I'm not a child, and haven't been one for many years now. I know the apartment I've found is the right one for me. It's clean, reasonably priced, and close to where I work."

Glorene's eyes were flashing. "You wouldn't even *have* that job if I hadn't introduced you to Creighton. And he wouldn't have the stables if I hadn't worked the sale with Blackburn!"

Kassie tensed. "You don't have to tell me that. I'm aware..."

But Glorene refused to listen. "And I thought you said good old Grandpa wanted us to be together. If so, then he meant together, not apart."

"He said to come to Virginia to be with you. I don't interpret that to mean living in the same residence."

"And why not?" her sister snapped. "If you move way out by Blackburn's, you might just as well be back in

128

Wyoming. So why don't you just pack up and go back to the cow country?"

Kassie studied her sister's angry face. Had Glorene been making life difficult for her to try to drive her back to Wyoming? The thought was disturbing. "We can still see one another," she said. "That is, if we *want* to."

"And what about Leomia?" Glorene continued as though Kassie hadn't spoken. "I thought you liked her. Are you going to run off from her too? Is that the way a Christian is supposed to act—to leave the people who have helped you the most?"

"The way this Christian acts is to obey the voice of God speaking to my heart. And that's what I intend to do."

"Oh, go on and move out, if that's what you want. See if I care. Who needs you? But let me tell you something. If you lose that job and fall flat, don't come crying to me." Savagely, she crushed out the cigarette in the ash tray. "And I won't help you move either. You want to be on your own—then just do it." With exaggerated steps, she fetched her blazer and her purse from the bedroom and slammed out of the apartment.

Kassie wasted no time in starting to pack. Leomia stayed over to join in and lend a hand. The kindly housekeeper obviously was attempting to make up for Glorene's attack.

At the stables the next day, Kassie explained her predicament to Harlis, and that evening he sent Travis and Wooster to load up her few boxes of belongings, to take them to the friendly old house on Williamette Boulevard. Kassie dreaded another confrontation with her sister, especially in front of the boys, but Glorene never appeared. Not even to say good-bye.

Leomia didn't seem at all surprised by Kassie's decision to leave. When she learned the address, she was delighted. "That's near where my daughter lives," she said. "I'll come and visit you now and then to see how you're doing. And don't worry about Glorene. She'll calm down soon. Just keep praying for her." Leomia almost smothered her with a big hug. "You'll be just fine."

Mom Tinsley greeted them at the front door, and instructed them to back the pickup into the driveway. To the boys she said, "You may take Kassie's things upstairs now, but after this," she shook a thin finger at them, "I want you to know you must obey the rules and call for her in the parlor *only*."

Travis and Wooster glanced at one another and tried to muffle their explosions of giggles. Pushing the boxes into Kassie's little kitchen, they cracked jokes about Mom Tinsley being Mother Superior. Kassie joined in the laughter, because regardless of how Mom sounded to them, she was deliriously happy.

Out the tall living room windows, she looked down upon a back yard full of flowers. Fat pink peonies, scarlet roses, and rainbows of irises. Not structured and formal like Ronson Gardens, but homey. Oh, so homey. And that's what she'd been starved for all these months.

In the ensuing days, the five employees at Blackburn's were harder pressed than ever as the business began to pick up. In a conference with Creighton, they outlined schedules for riding lessons to be offered for all ages. Eagerly, Kassie agreed to teach a beginner class of children once a week on Thursday afternoons.

Now in order to volunteer at the hospital, she had to catch a bus near her apartment and ride back downtown.

Perhaps by this time next year, she would have her own car.

One evening when she arrived at McKinley, she was met by a grinning Holly. "You're to report to eighth floor right away," she instructed.

"What's up?" Holly never looked that cheerful usually when she spoke of Lexi.

"You'll see. Just get on up there."

Kassie stepped off the elevator, expecting as usual to enter a darkened room. When she entered a brightly lit room with a lady fully dressed, sitting at the desk, she thought she'd made a mistake. "Oh, excuse me. I'm terribly... Lexi?"

"Yes, my dear. It's me." She put her hands to the gray hair which was still quite straggled. "What's left of me anyway."

"But you're..."

"Up and dressed. Yes. And I've opened the drapes and even watered the poor desperate plants. Come in, Kassie, and sit down." The dark-rimmed eyes were smiling ever so slightly.

Kassie was so in shock, she wondered that she could even walk to the chair. She stepped inside in a daze. "I'm so thankful you're better. Tell me what's happened."

"It's because of you and little Mindy, and the God you both serve." She opened the desk drawer. "Look at this." There was a mound of paper scraps.

"What are those?"

"Notes from Mindy. Jokes, riddles, Scripture verses, prayers. You name it, it's there." The angular lines of her face softened. "Listen to this one." She unfolded a little piece of notebook paper. "'Knock, knock,' she writes to me. I answer 'Who's there?' Back comes 'Oswald.' So I write back, 'Oswald who?' Then I got the punch line, 'Oswald my gum.'" And the mystery lady who'd been buried in a dark room for weeks gave a little giggle. "Isn't that wonderful?"

Kassie shook her head. "How'd she manage all this?"

"You brought the first note, remember? The one that got me out of bed to watch the horse show. I saw you ride, Kassie. You were great. It was *all* great. I just couldn't get over all those little children out there." Slowly, she rose to move toward the bed, her movement stiff and stilted. "After that, she used the aides and volunteers as message bearers. It's been going hot and heavy for the last two days."

She sat on the bed and leaned heavily against the pillows. "Mindy explained to me the simplicity of the Gospel, and even sent me a little tract." Tears welled up in Lexi's eyes. "For the first time, I really understood that Jesus died for me and that I could accept Him as my personal Savior. I'm a Christian now, Kassie."

"Oh Lexi, what a miracle."

"After your visits, the Scripture you'd read would roll over and over in my mind, haunting me. Thank you for caring enough to read to me. Yesterday, I asked Jesus into my heart just like the tract said." She pulled a tissue from the box by the bed and dabbed at her eyes and blew her nose. "I feel all clean inside."

Kassie went to the bed and gave her friend a hug. She couldn't stop her own tears, and yet the two of them were laughing at the same time. Kassie knew she would never forget this moment.

They pulled out the Bible and pored over the Scriptures

until Kassie had to leave. Lexi was unfamiliar with much of the Bible and had an abundance of questions.

As Kassie was leaving, Lexi called after her, "I'll take you up on that offer to fix my hair."

"Next time," Kassie promised. "We'll do it up real spiffy."

Kassie couldn't wait to ask Mindy all about the details of the notes and share with her the good news, but Holly intercepted her in the main lobby.

"Well, what do you think?" she asked, bright-eyed.

"It's the most glorious miracle I've ever seen, outside of when my Grandpa Carver accepted Christ. I'm thrilled."

"Do you have a minute? Lexi's doctor wants to talk with you."

"Lexi's doctor? Whatever for?"

"Just some general questions, I'm sure. He can meet you in the conference room just down the hall. Then you can go see the kids, which I'm sure is where you want to be." They exchanged the warm knowing smiles of good friends.

Lexi's doctor was a slender, middle-aged man, with thinning hair and a trim mustache. He was brief and to the point. "You've seen the stark change in Lexi, I hear," he said after they were comfortably seated.

"Yes, sir. It's wonderful."

"We have you to thank for some of this development, I believe."

"A little girl in pediatrics did most of it." Kassie wasn't trying to be overly modest. Mindy's notes and letters had turned the tide.

"And I'm told you introduced them—sort of."

"Yes." Kassie wondered if she'd done something wrong.

"I'm also told Lexi thinks a lot of you, and because of that, I've called you in here to ask a favor. A rather unorthodox favor, I'm afraid."

Kassie smoothed the skirt of her pink uniform. "I'll be glad to do what I can."

"Lexi, it would seem, is ready to leave the hospital. However, my associates and I are not sure she's ready to be with her family just yet. She needs a place to stay—away from the temptations of alcohol. She needs a friend. Holly tells us that you've recently moved into your own apartment outside the metroplex. Could Lexi stay with you for a short time, Miss Carver? Until we can determine the extent of her ability to adjust to new surroundings?"

This sounded like a terribly big step, and a great responsibility. Yet, Kassie immediately knew this was what she was to do. Mom Tinsley might even help keep Lexi company while Kassie was at work. Between them, they could get her into a church.

"We'll have to ask you to shield her from others for a time," the doctor went on. "Because of her family. You understand, don't you?"

Kassie didn't understand. She never had understood. But even if she had to keep Lexi hidden, she knew the answer was yes. No church. No other friends. "What about my landlady? She's a precious Christian lady who could be a friend to Lexi while I'm at work. And she'll need to know that someone else is in the apartment with me."

The doctor rubbed at his mustache as he thought. "You're right. Yes, the landlady. But please, no one else. Not yet anyway."

thirteen

Mom Tinsley and Lexi hit it off immediately. Theirs was a friendship obviously made in heaven. When Kassie left for work each day, Mom went upstairs to keep Lexi company. Often they worked out back in the flower beds. Sometimes they made chocolate chip cookies in Kassie's sunny kitchen. Whatever they did, Mom Tinsley was careful to interject discussions about God's love. Each day when Kassie returned, Lexi's face glowed more.

The day before the overnight trail ride, two special extra-long horse trailers were brought in to transport the horses to Weller's Cove. Some clients had their own horses and planned to meet at the cove. Others were renting mounts from the stables, and Blackburn's small crew was responsible for getting both stock and tack to the location safely and on time.

Loren and Harlis had masterminded most of the details for the outing, with Creighton adding a suggestion here and there. They were to ride the trails along the beach of the inlet for several miles, then through the stands of forest to the juncture where the peninsula jutted out. This vast sandy beach area at the edge of the tree line was to be the evening campsite. The following day they would travel down the length of the peninsula to the lighthouse point, then ferry back to their starting point.

After the last stubborn equine was loaded in the trailers, Kassie was given a hand up into the truck cab by

Travis. There she was pressed against Loren's side as Travis piled in beside her. Harlis was driving the other truck.

The drive from the stables to Weller's Cove took about an hour. Loren's deep dimples flashed as he ground through the truck gears and cracked truck driver jokes with Travis. Indeed he could have passed for an ordinary truck driver with his soft knit shirt open at the neck, contouring over the muscular chest and shoulders.

Bright sunshine spilled into the cab, and Kassie basked in the delicious cozy sensation of Loren's nearness and the aroma of his spicy cologne. Drowsily, she studied the dark tangle of hair on his forearm, and quietly gave thanks that he seemed so relaxed today. The tightness was gone from the tanned face.

Several families were already assembled at the appointed starting place when the Blackburn crew arrived. Clusters of horse trailers were parked in a grove of trees. The excited laughter of children rang through the trees as they engaged in a spontaneous game of tag.

Kassie allowed Loren to reach up and help her down out of the cab. She touched the ground, but his hands held to her waist. Looking up at him, his sky blue eyes seemed clearer and more translucent than ever before. "Now you'll see what I mean, Kassie. You'll love the ocean by horseback."

"Thanks for making it possible," she answered, her thinking once again fuzzied by his touch.

His lips kissed the sunshine warmth of the top of her hair. "My pleasure, Kassie," he whispered. "My pleasure." His words slid down over her like a delicious caress.

"Hey there, you two," Travis shouted. "Let's get this

show on the road."

Loren gave a soft chuckle. "We're discovered. Guess we'd better get busy."

Kassie had little time to think about Loren after that moment. While the guys worked with the mounts, she organized the participants, patiently explaining procedures and rules and helping them to pack their gear correctly. A brown-eyed four-year-old named Danny quickly attached himself to her and announced that he wanted his horse to ride beside hers.

She and Loren were reviewing the time schedules when Sean drove up, pulling a brand new horse trailer, which housed his new mount. He looked like a kid on Christmas morning with a new toy.

Loren's expression clouded as he glanced up and saw Sean. "Don't look now, Miss Muffet," he remarked, "but Spiderman's here."

"Loren," she reprimanded. "Don't be hateful."

"Who's being hateful? I just never did build up a liking for spiders." He made several quick checks on the sheets of paper in the clipboard and handed it back to her. "Who invited him anyway?"

"He was at the grand opening and saw the sign up sheet. It *is* open to everyone, isn't it?"

"Everyone but spiders," he answered. "Travis!"

"Yeah?"

"Help the greenhorn get unloaded, will you?" He nodded toward Sean.

"Sure thing," Travis called back.

"That's all we need," Loren muttered, "a novice. These children here know more about riding than Phipps does."

"He's been doing pretty good at the stables," Kassie

said, feeling she should defend poor Sean, who'd come in a few times for trail rides.

"Pretty good may not be good enough out here," he quipped before walking away.

Everything Loren had said about enjoying the ocean by horseback was true and more. The restful rocking of the loping horses blended with the gentle roll and swell of the splashing waves. The clear sky, dotted with only a few blue-edged clouds, stretched endlessly above them, blending with the ocean's horizon in the far distance. Kassie wished she were alone and could allow Regalia to race down the beach at a hard gallop.

Loren was at the head of the line, directing and guiding the long line of riders. Travis and Wooster brought up the rear, and Kassie stayed in the midst of the group, mostly with the children, but always beside the wide-eyed Danny who constantly maneuvered his pony to be in close proximity.

She could tell by the look on Sean's face he wanted to be near her. Unexplainably, she felt herself avoiding him.

By mid-day, the riders were well acquainted, laughing, talking, and enjoying one another's company. Kassie realized these people could become close riding friends, who would enjoy coming to the stables to be together. From a business aspect, this was a great concept. She wanted very much to see the stables grow and be successful. At times, she could scarcely believe she was being paid for doing what she loved the most.

At the noon campsite, over a lunch of sandwiches, Harlis announced that evening thunder squalls had been predicted. He was speaking to Loren, but Kassie overheard.

Reading concern in Harlis' leathery face, she stepped

over to where they were talking. "Do we cancel the over-night stay?" she wanted to know.

Loren looked at her with surprise. "No need for that. The tents are waterproof. No problem."

She glanced at Harlis. He shrugged his bony shoulders and walked off.

The sun continued to shine across the gleaming, glit-tering waves, in blinding diamond sparkles. Later that afternoon their trail took them inland, weaving in and out among the trees. The group grew quiet as they soaked in the magnificent beauty of the dense, cool forest. The lapping of the waves grew fainter, and bird calls and the rustling of the wind in the trees were the only sounds.

Through the trees, Kassie could see Loren sitting tall and straight in the saddle. As though he felt her gaze, he turned around and gave her the fullest, most relaxed smile she'd ever seen, and a new light came on deep within her.

❧

Travis poked at the dying embers of the campfire with a long stick, sending a fresh spray of glowing sparks shoot-ing up into the darkness. Kassie felt so full of supper's tasty fried fish, she thought she would burst. Harlis had turned out to be a marvelous camp cook. The children were quietly mumbling in their sleep, and most of the chattering of the adults was now quieted as well. Kassie had not stretched out before an evening campfire in a long time, and she found herself dwelling on sweet memories of her times out on the cattle drives with Grandpa.

A small tent city had been erected at the edge of the tree line, and the nickering horses were tethered in a clear-ing farther back in the woods.

Loren came and knelt down beside her. "We'd better

check the horses one more time before bedding down," he said.

Obediently, she followed the bobbing beam of his flashlight away from the glowing campfire. "How'd you and Regalia get along today?" he asked.

"Splendidly. She's perfect. Such a great disposition."

Methodically, they checked halter ropes on each of the horses and calmed them with their quiet voices.

"There's a backwash pool up here," with his flashlight beam he pointed off through the trees, "surrounded by cypress and flowers." He held out his hand. "Want to see?"

Silently, she slipped her hand into his larger, strong one and walked along beside him. Muted moonlight bathed the backwash pool in a burnished orange color, and the crimson flowers glowed a fluorescent pink, giving the place a fairy land effect. The damp air was heavy with the fragrance of the ocean and the flowers.

Loren led her to the water's edge and plucked a wild flower and placed it in her hand. "For you."

"Thank you." She pressed the cool blossom to her cheek. "This is beautiful."

"Better than Wyoming?"

She smiled. "You've obviously never seen the Grand Tetons or Yellowstone."

"If not better, gentler perhaps? Not so rugged?"

"Only if there are no alligators in the swamps."

"Hey, it's not swampy here."

"I hope you're right. I'm afraid of quicksand too."

Loren pulled her to face him. "Would you get serious?"

"I'm trying."

"Maybe this will help." Gently he enfolded her and molded her to himself, bathing her with kisses which burned deep—deep inside to where the light had come on. Kassie responded in a yielded giving that she knew was too reckless, that she was certain he sensed.

"Kassie, Kassie." The words were in her hair, in her ear, down across her neck. "I've never known any girl like you. Wonderful sweet Kassie. I can't get my mind off you. I look for you in a crowd. I listen for your voice. I dream of you at night."

Kassie's heart was pounding in her temples. She began to push away. "Please, Loren, not so fast." For so long she had questioned and wondered, not knowing. But now... "We need to slow down. Take our time." She sought her breath and forced it back to its regular rhythm.

"Time? What does time matter? Let's not waste any more precious time."

"But Loren..." Her mind was a wild war of confusion.

"I know you feel the same about me. I can feel it when you're near me."

"Yes..." She heard the hesitation in her own voice.

"Then what is it?"

"The Lord..." she began, but he wouldn't let her finish. He stepped back. "Don't, Kassie. Please don't."

"But it's so important to me."

"God has no part in this. No part. This is you and I. Here and now. In the reality of life. I'm telling you that I care deeply about you, and you want to toss God in the center and make it a triangle." Loren leaned his weight against a nearby tree trunk. "I can't compete against God for your love."

Kassie searched desperately for the right words. For Loren to confess to her that he cared was something she had never dared to hope for, but something she had longed for. But for him to misunderstand about God's love was agonizing to her. "Can't you see, Loren, everything I am, that which you say you care for, is because of God and His love? You needn't compete against God, but join me in my love for Him."

"When we were kids, Roger and I went everywhere together." Loren broke off a dead twig and began breaking off small pieces as he spoke. "That often included church, Sunday school classes, even Bible school in the summer. But then in high school, something changed. All of a sudden, Roger was always in church, always had his nose in the Bible, always was spouting Scriptures. It was like an obsession. A gulf grew between us as wide as that ocean out there." He waved toward the beach area. "I don't want to go through that again."

"God loves you, Loren. Can't you see that?"

Loren shook his head. "If He loved me, He never would have let Roger die, and our father be spared. Or else He would have seen to it that *I* was in that plane in Roger's place. Roger deserved to live."

Before she could counter his remarks, he went on. "Dad still owns Jolly Roger. Roger was in the process of buying him when he died. He loved that horse, so Dad used him for leverage like he's doing now. That horse will be mine only if I win the Jumper Classic. That's Dad's stipulation. Otherwise he'll sell him. I've got to get that horse and keep him for Roger's sake. I've got to do that for him."

She nodded. The scheme sounded like something Vaughn would do—going out of his way to make life miserable for others, even his own son. "You can do that for Roger," she said. "Get Jolly Roger by winning, finish law school, and be what Roger dreamed of being. But for what?" She stepped closer to him. "Roger's gone, Loren. He's with the Lord, enjoying the wonders of heaven. If he were talking to you right now, he'd tell you nothing in this life is as important as your relationship with the Father."

Loren threw down the stick in his hand and stepped forward to grip her arms. "Kassie, do you love me?" His fingers were tight as though trying to squeeze the answer from her.

"Yes, Loren." She hadn't been sure before. But this afternoon during the ride, when he had looked back at her and she had seen what he could become... She looked at him now, still so very handsome and yet with tension holding him in its clutches. Nevertheless, she knew. "I do love you."

His grasp relaxed. His arms enclosed her. "Then you'll back off on this religious stuff? For me? Let me be the one in your life?"

She lay her head against the broad chest, savoring the sweetness of it, knowing the pain of what she must say. Until they served the same One, it could never be. "I can't do that, Loren. Not for you or anyone."

"But if you love someone..." He pulled away again.

"If my faith had a price, if you could buy me out, one day you'd hate me."

At first, Kassie thought it was the wind in the trees she heard. A cooler wind was blowing now, and an occasional soft flash of far-off lightning. But the rustling grew louder. It was someone moving through the underbrush toward them.

"Gracious me!" Sean said with a wide grin on his face.

"I sure didn't know you folks were out this way. I was just taking a short walk. I couldn't sleep."

"Quite all right." Loren's voice had gone cold. "We were just finished."

૱

The rain began lightly at first, barely pelting the tents with a lullaby rhythm. Kassie shared a tent with one of the young girls, and she listened, hoping the drumming would drum out memories of her conversation with Loren and put her to sleep. But she kept reliving every moment she'd ever spent with him, wondering when he had first discovered his love for her.

In the pre-dawn hours the wind began to blow and drive the rain harder. She wasn't sure she had slept at all. But she was certainly deep in sleep when she first heard Loren calling her name.

"Kassie! Wake up, Kassie!"

Through a fog of sleep, she roused to know she wasn't dreaming. With great effort, she opened the front flap and was greeted with a face full of driving rain.

Loren was draped in his rain poncho. "We'll have to pull out right away. The storm's worsening. We can't wait it out. Saddle Regalia and help saddle the kids' horses." His voice held a note of urgency.

She obeyed without a word, thankful that she always packed rain gear. Some of the others, she was sure, had not. The rain was like a monsoon. People were stirring about. The men were hurriedly taking down tents. Loren had assigned her to the horses, because that was what she could do the best—that and calming the children.

With little panic or problem, they were soon in their line ready to pull out. The plan was to re-track, rather than move down the peninsula. Crossing on the ferries would be impossible in the storm.

Little Danny, still half asleep, was placed in the saddle with her, and she tucked him under her ample poncho, relishing the warmth of his little body against hers.

The dawn, through the storm-wracked skies, was barely giving enough light for them to make out the way through the dense trees. Blinding flashes of lightning gave the horses a bad case of jitters. They had just rounded a curve, when suddenly the horse ahead of Regalia bolted at the crack of thunder, and the rider fought to regain control.

Regalia gave a nervous whinny and sidestepped sharply. When she did, Kassie felt herself slipping. She was helplessly falling through the air and precious Danny was falling with her. She remembered praying that she would not fall on top of him, then she felt the air being socked from her lungs. For an agonizing moment of time, her body forgot how to breathe. Why no other horses ever stepped on them, she could only wonder.

Danny was crying in lusty sobs. Others dismounted and gathered about. Then Loren was there kneeling down beside her. Other than being unable to catch her breath, she seemed to be all in one piece. Danny, badly frightened, was also unhurt. Quickly, he was given over to his mother, who quieted his crying. Loren instructed the others to remount and go on.

Kassie was helped to her feet, and Loren brought Regalia to her. "The cinch, Kassie." His voice was tense. "You forgot to tighten Regalia's cinch. And I was worried about Phipps. You could have caused mass panic here with these horses."

She looked squarely at Loren's rain-drenched face. "I've

been riding too long to forget to tighten a cinch, Loren. It *was* tightened. Securely." Pains jabbed her chest as she spoke. She ignored it. "Someone had to have loosened it."

Suddenly she remembered the words of Vaughn Marcellus: "I'll go to any length..." Kassie realized with a shudder that he could have hired anyone in the group to loosen that cinch. Both she and Danny could have been badly hurt. Or killed.

Loren was now totally exasperated. "You sound as paranoid as your sister. Why blame someone else for your own carelessness?"

"And you sound as heartless as your father. You should have turned this group back yesterday when you first heard the storm warnings."

Hadn't Vaughn tried to tell her? "We're profoundly alike," he had said. Well, she should have listened. Angrily, she wheeled about to tighten the cinch. She hoped this embarrassing incident had not caused their clients to lose faith in them.

As she set herself to remount, Sean was there by her side. "Here, Kassie, let me help." He didn't even have a hat on. And only a light jacket. "Are you sure you're all right?"

"Thanks, Sean. I'll be fine." Bodily she was fine, other than a few bruises. But who could heal her broken heart?

Gently, Sean helped lift her into the saddle and smiled up at her. As best she could, she returned a smile of gratitude.

fourteen

Loren spent less time at the stables now. His workouts with Jolly Roger were either late at night or very early in the morning. Harlis told Kassie it was because he was approaching finals week at the university, but she knew that wasn't the truth. He was avoiding her.

Kassie determined not to let her hurt feelings hinder her work at Blackburn's. No matter what happened in her personal life, her job was too important not to do her best each day. Working with the stable's clients had become one of her greatest joys. And the children's classes were her delight. And Harlis and the boys had become great friends to her—almost like family.

Each day, she could see the success of the business growing as she balanced the accounts. Creighton showered them with praise as he observed the steady rate of growth and called Kassie often to ask for updated information.

Several of those who had been on the trail ride told her they felt Loren had been too hard on her. Surprisingly, she defended his actions. "A leader," she insisted, "must also be a disciplinarian."

Danny's mother had been kind and understanding. And brown-eyed Danny, who was now her student, held no grudges either. Only Loren, it seemed, still blamed her—for everything.

Now that Lexi was living with her, Kassie had no time to volunteer at the hospital, so when Holly called her late one evening, Kassie was excited to hear her voice.

"Holly, I'm so glad you called. I've missed you so much. How is everyone? What's Mindy been up to?"

"That's why I called." Kassie detected the catch in her friend's voice. "Mindy passed away this afternoon."

Kassie let out a little gasp and slowly lowered herself into the wicker chair by the tall living room windows. "Oh, Holly. No." She was overwhelmed by a sense of loss for the little girl she'd known only a short time. Tears flowed freely down her cheeks. Dear, precious Mindy. Everyone who'd met her had loved her. Lexi walked in from the kitchen and saw Kassie's face. "It's Mindy, isn't it?" she whispered.

Kassie nodded, then listened as Holly gave details of the funeral arrangements. "Thank you, Holly." Her own voice sounded far away, as though it were echoing in a hollow drum. "I think I have the directions straight. I'll see you there."

Kassie and Lexi wept together for the little child who had been an integral part of their friendship. A deep ache washed over Kassie, when suddenly she realized she was weeping not only for Mindy, but also for her loss of Loren as well. For almost two weeks, she'd moved about in limbo, not allowing her mind to dwell on him.

"Kassie!" Mom Tinsley's squeaky voice called from the stairs. "A visitor for you."

As best she could, Kassie nursed the redness from her eyes with cold water and hurried into the hall hoping against hope that her visitor might be Loren.

Instead, Sean was grinning at her as he stood leaning against the banister. He sobered at the sight of her tear-swollen eyes. "Kassie, are you all right? What's wrong?"

Kassie descended from the landing and allowed Sean to embrace her. He'd been so kind to her, and now the reassurance of his arms eased the hurting. "It's little Mindy. The girl at McKinley that I told you about. She died today." Hot tears began to flow again.

He held her tight. "I'm so sorry, Kassie. I know how much you loved her. Would it help if you went somewhere? A walk in the park? A drive? Ronson Gardens?"

She shook her head. "Thanks, Sean. That's kind of you, but I still have other things that must be done around here."

"Can I pick you up and take you to the funeral?"

"I'm not sure. I'll call and let you know."

Just then, Lexi stepped down to the landing. "Kassie, dear? Telephone for you."

"Oh, thank you." She turned back to Sean. "I'll have to go now. But thanks for coming by."

"Sure, Kassie. I'm here for you. Call if you need me." He nodded toward the stairs. "She a friend of yours?"

She nodded and started to pull away, but he drew her close and kissed her soundly. How ironic that she'd once pushed him away. Now even though she indulged him, she felt guilty, as though she were using him. She pulled away and hurried up the stairs.

The call was only Harlis double checking with her about class schedules. She answered his questions, then told him about Mindy's death, explaining that she would have to be away from the office the day of the funeral. Hanging up the phone, she scolded herself for constantly hoping that each call, each visitor might be Loren.

Later that night, after Lexi was sleeping peacefully on the living room daybed, Kassie made up her mind to call

Loren. He needed to know about Mindy. He'd been quite taken with her.

Nervously, she picked up the phone in her bedroom. When he answered, she nearly panicked. "Loren? This is Kassie." Her heart was triple-beating at the sound of his voice.

"Yes, Kassie? What do you need?" His voice was business-like. Reserved.

"I thought you would want to know..." She couldn't speak. Her voice was frozen.

"Know what?"

"About Mindy."

"At the hospital?"

"Yes."

"What about her?" His voice was tighter now.

"She's fine now, Loren." A spasm caught her throat. "She went to be with the Lord today."

"With the Lord? Another plastic Christian phrase? You mean she died, right?"

"Please. It's difficult enough. She's whole now. Complete with Him."

"That's what the preacher tried to tell me when Roger died. It's a handful of air, and doesn't do a thing for the gut-wrenching pain. Spare me the religious talk. I'll tackle life in my *own* way."

When she took a breath to answer, the slam of the receiver crashed in her ear.

Sleep came fitfully that night. She couldn't remember a time when she was any more restless. At last she simply rose to pace the floor and pour out her heart to the Lord. Seeking His presence and His will was all she knew to do. The peace that came was fortifying—but even that could not have prepared her for the early morning visitor she received.

After only an hour or two of sleep, she was awakened by one of the other tenants, rapping softly on her door. "A lady downstairs to see you, Kassie."

"A lady? Thanks. I'll be right down." By the time Kassie slipped into her robe, Lexi was roused. Though dawn had barely broken, she offered to start the morning coffee.

When Kassie turned at the landing, she caught sight of a grim, white-faced Glorene, pacing the floral carpet in the parlor. "Glorene, I'm so glad you're here. Please come up and see my little home."

Glorene whirled on her. "You little vixen! I take you in, feed you, let you sleep under my roof, and what do you do in thanks? Double-cross me—and all of us!"

Kassie felt her knees go weak. She clung to the banister. "Double-cross? I don't know what you're talking about."

"Don't give me that garbage. How much did they pay you? First you hide her out in your cozy little apartment, then you let the story leak two days before the election. Vaughn must have paid you a pretty penny for that."

"Glorene, stop it! Slow down! You're not making any sense."

Furious now, Glorene shook a newspaper in Kassie's face. "Here! Take a look at what the vultures at the Gazette did with your story."

Kassie took the paper and stared at the scathing head-lines: *Sister of Campaign Manager Hides Hollister's Alcoholic Wife for Dry-Out.* The article took up the sordid refrain. "It is as yet uncertain whether or not the young attractive sister of Glorene Paquette was in fact put on the

Hollister payroll to keep his wife, who suffered with bouts of depression, alcoholism, and suicidal tendencies, under wraps and out of his way until after the election..."

Waves of nausea spread over Kassie. "Lexi is Creighton's wife?"

Glorene gave a sad, empty laugh. "Great show, Baby. But you can drop it now. No academy awards for this one. But it was a good try. You come breezing into town playing Miss Purity to the hilt, and all the time you're crafty enough to play both ends against the middle." Her eyes were gaunt and hollow. "Thanks, little sister, for coming along just in time to foul up my only chance at happiness. I bet you and good old Alexandria had a million laughs about it."

"Glorene, I had no idea..."

Glorene put up her hands. "Save it for the press. You're gonna need it." She glanced at her watch. "I'm surprised they haven't been here before now. You'd better hope Creighton gets here first."

"Creighton?" Her mind was reeling.

"I'm leaving before they get here." She stopped with her hand on the front door knob. "Too bad good old Grandpa isn't here so I could thank him for sending you my way. Thank God he's not around to do me any more favors—like sending a package of rattlesnakes." The slamming door rattled the window panels on either side.

Kassie stood still for a moment, then slowly ascended the stairs.

Lexi was humming a little tune as she set out the cups and saucers on the table. She looked up as Kassie entered. She gave a slow half-smile. "You know?"

"Yes. I guess everyone knows." She laid the newspaper

out on the table.

Lexi winced at the savage headlines. "Someone found out I was here and used it to their advantage. Must have made a pretty penny out of it."

"The press thinks Creighton paid me to keep you out of the way, and my sister thinks I took money from the Bosworth camp to break the story at the right time. What a mess."

"Poor Kassie." She stepped over and put her arms around Kassie and gave her a comforting hug. "I should have told you the truth after I arrived here. After I learned that you were working for Creighton. But it would have been more difficult for you had you known.

"Actually Creighton *was* hiding me," Lexi explained. "But it was for my sake, not his. I was hoping to make the grand announcement of my recovery to the press on my own very soon, but I had to be sure I was ready. If Creighton becomes the mayor of Westport, I had to be prepared to face the temptations of alcohol again. But with your help and Mom Tinsley's, my confidence is soaring."

They were interrupted by Mom Tinsley at the door, though usually she simply called from the bottom of the stairs. Kassie opened the door.

"Against all house procedures," she said with a smile and a twinkle in her eye, "I'm allowing a man on the second floor today." She waved a skinny arm and Creighton appeared in the darkened hallway.

Lexi gasped. "Creighton!" Like a young girl, she flung herself into his open arms. Desperately, they clung to one another.

"Alexandria, you're all right. I can't believe you're all right again." He held her away from him for a moment and simply gazed at her face.

Now Kassie knew what Glorene probably suspected all along—that Creighton had never stopped loving his wife. A pang of sorrow for her sister welled up into a knot of pain inside her.

"We were just having coffee," Kassie announced. "Mom and Creighton, won't you join us?"

Mom Tinsley gave a happy little laugh. "This is the best thing that's happened in this old house for many a year. And I'm as full of curiosity as a little kitten. But I'll rein it in and leave you all to your privacy." She chuckled again. "I'll guard the front door. The whole town'll be here before you know it." She turned to go. "Kassie, you can tell me all the rich details later."

Over coffee, Creighton couldn't take his eyes off Lexi. "All the doctors would tell me is that you were in good hands, and that you were improving. But I was so afraid to hope. I can't believe you were here with Kassie all the time. How marvelous!"

In bits and pieces, the two ladies filled him in on the details of the past few weeks, including Mindy's part and her death.

Finally, Kassie had to ask, "Creighton, do you think I took payment to spill the story to the press this close to the election?"

"Kassie Carver, I could never think such a thing about you. But it's obvious someone timed it pretty close. You have any idea who?"

Kassie hadn't even taken time to think about it, but as soon as Creighton asked, a sickening knowledge came over her. "I think I do now."

"Want to say?" he asked.

"Not yet."

The press and TV newsmen converged on the house before the morning was out, and Mom Tinsley enjoyed every minute of it. She dutifully gave each and every one of them Creighton's message that he would hold a press conference that afternoon at campaign headquarters.

Later, when the coast was clear, Creighton and Lexi loaded her things in his car and left, showering Kassie and Mom Tinsley with hugs of thanksgiving.

When all was quiet again, Kassie went to her phone and dialed Sean.

His "hello" sounded cautious.

"You sold out to Vaughn Marcellus, didn't you, Sean?" She was startled by her own brashness.

She heard his nervous laugh on the other end. "Kassie, there's enough in this for both of us."

An involuntary shiver clutched her. "You never needed money. You're a Quillian. Remember?"

"Money? Oh, Kassie. Little Kassie, so totally sweet and innocent. Money is only a small part of it. Power, position, and another rung up in the city political structure. All types of little favors. It's going to be such fun. I want to share all the glory with you, Kassie. I'm going places in Westport. Who knows, maybe one day I'll be running for state senator!"

"And if Bosworth loses?"

"Not a chance now."

"Now that the whole city thinks Creighton hid his own wife while he was campaigning?"

"Hey, I didn't *plan* to see his wife at your apartment that day. It was just a glorious stroke of luck. And when I realized you didn't even know who she was, that made it even better. Old Marcellus was getting pretty impatient when I kept feeding him Mickey Mouse information. But when I had that kind of news, they all sat up and took notice of me."

"What about Regalia's cinch the night of the storm?"

"Oh, honey. You know Vaughn. He insisted I scare you a little on that trip. I had to convince him I meant business for his side. How was I to know you'd have the kid with you? I knew you'd never get hurt in a fall like that. You're an expert with horses. But forget all that. Let's look at the future, you and me..."

She didn't slam the receiver down. She simply eased down the receiver button with her finger and held it there. "So you knew I wouldn't get hurt, did you? How thoughtful." And yet she could feel no anger toward him. Only pity. Pity for such a pathetic person who would soon be crushed in Bosworth's gargantuan political machine. He may have sold out to them, but he would never be ruthless enough to survive the system he'd been sucked into. Perhaps all the Quillian business would go down with him.

At the afternoon news conference, Creighton made clear that he had not paid anyone to keep Lexi hidden. But Kassie knew with all the mud-slinging, many people wouldn't believe him. Bosworth's people were already issuing a sordid variety of stories, capitalizing on the event.

That next week, Creighton and Lexi came to pick Kassie up to go to Mindy's funeral. Seeing the two of them together, Kassie could almost make herself forget Glorene's harsh anger and resentment.

The funeral was a praise service made up of Christian families in a small church outside Westport. In spite of their grief, the family and friends plainly knew well that death was not the end, but merely a graduation.

Kassie was startled at one point to glance back and see Loren's massive frame, dressed in a pale blue three-piece business suit, leaning against the back wall. Someone offered him a seat, but he shook his head. His light brown wavy hair was brushed softly back. He was even more incredibly handsome than Kassie could ever remember. Eons seemed to have passed since the night they'd stood together by the moonlit backwash.

Before the message was given by the pastor, Mindy's young mother walked with head erect to the platform. She did not try to stop the tears, nor did she let the tears stop her words. "Time here on earth," she said, "is but a speck of dust in comparison to eternity. And Mindy's father and I know we shall be with Mindy for eternity one day. Our moment of reuniting is in the wings. Only a breath away."

Kassie looked back again. Loren was gone.

fifteen

"Are you going to watch the election returns with us here at headquarters?" Creighton was looking at Kassie with those gentle eyes of his. They were seated in his office at headquarters and he was giving her a few last minute calls to make. Now that Lexi had moved back home, Kassie had begun her volunteer work again.

She shook her head. "I don't think that's a good idea. Glorene's still so hurt. I seem to multiply that hurt when I'm around her. She's convinced that if it weren't for me, she would have had you for her own."

"I've tried to talk to her," Creighton said, "but she clams up." He slid a finger under the knot in his tie and pulled it loose. The day had been long—and so had the campaign. "Much of the blame is mine. I should never have openly shared my problems with her. It was obvious to me she cared about me, but I was too blind to see it had grown into more than that. If I'd put a stop to it early on, the two of you might not be alienated now."

Kassie sighed. She halfway agreed with him. But who was she to be blaming? She was still punishing herself for playing so stupidly into Sean's manipulative hands. What irony, that while Glorene thought Kassie had pulled Sean into the Hollister camp, Kassie had actually given him the opportunity to glean information from her and feed it to Mayor Bosworth and Vaughn Marcellus.

"We don't know that it would have made any difference, Creighton. She loves you very much." Because of her own loss of Loren, Kassie could even relate to her sister's heartbreak in losing Creighton. Glorene had ignored the fact that Creighton was a married man, but Kassie had likewise ignored the fact that Loren wasn't a committed Christian. Which was the more foolish?

Creighton looked at her with eyes misting. "I had prepared myself for the fact that Lexi might never be well again. But she's so different now. You've restored to me my wife from years past. And yet she's even more vibrant and lovely than she was back then."

Kassie smiled. "She is lovely, isn't she? It's God's power of restoration. Thank Him."

The silver-haired executive leaned forward in his chair and rested his hands on the desk. "I've been giving that a lot of thought as well, Kassie. I've decided even if I lose the election tomorrow, I'm still a winner!"

❧

Kassie planned to rest that evening and simply listen to the returns on the radio. But before the polls were closed, Leomia arrived at Kassie's door toting a portable TV set under her arm. "I know you don't have a TV yet," she said. "So break out the popcorn and we'll watch together."

Kassie laughed. "Unless it's a landslide victory, they may not announce the results until the wee hours."

Leomia moved her hefty body right on in the door. "So? I'll curl up on the daybed and sack out. Something told me you needed company tonight."

"What about Glorene?"

"She's at headquarters. Gave me the night off."

"Oh, Leomia, you're such a dear." Kassie hugged her. "You were right, I need you very much."

Later that night, nearly midnight, she and Leomia heard persistent voices downstairs. "Mom Tinsley never allows anyone in this late." Kassie stood up and stretched. She'd nearly fallen asleep. "Must be another snoopy reporter. They've given me no rest in two days. I'll go down and give her a hand."

In the parlor, Mom Tinsley was face to face with a very tall, almost skinny gentleman. "Now look here," Kassie lashed out impatiently. "We're not giving out any more stories..." Her mouth fell open. "Ted?"

"There you are, Kassie. I tried to make this here fine lady understand that I knew you."

"Ted, what on earth are you doing in Westport?"

"Who is this man?" Mom Tinsley held onto her pert little robe which was neatly wrapped around her thin body.

"I'm sorry, Mom. This is Ted Winters, from my home town—the one who bought my grandfather's ranch. Ted, meet Mom Tinsley, my landlady."

"Pleased to meetcha." Ted extended a long arm.

"Land sakes." Mom Tinsley withdrew her attack position and returned his handclasp. "I guess since he's come so far, you can visit for a spell. In the parlor, of course. Then he's got to go. It is after hours, you know."

"Thanks, Mom. That'll be fine."

When they were alone, Kassie led him to the bench by the stairway where they both sat down. "I drove out to see the Royaliste Horse Show, Kassie," he explained. "I always wanted to see that thing, and when I realized it was Westport where you lived, I said, 'Well, why not?'"

"How in the world did you find me?"

"Mr. Norton at the bank had your address. He said you just moved to a new place. I hope you didn't mind my asking. He said you were still dealing with the home bank."

"I don't mind." She was, in fact, quite flattered.

"I guess I should have waited till morning, but I was as excited as a little kid. You glad to see me? You look prettier than ever."

"Yes, Ted, I'm very glad to see you." His voice, his aroma, his kind manner all fit together to kindle afresh the sparks of her homesickness. "Are the children with you?"

He shook his head. "They're with their grandma. It was too long a trip for them. Hey, I want to stay on the good side of the little banty hen there, so I'll leave and call you tomorrow. I'm at the Sheraton." He stepped toward her and reached for her hands. "Will you go to the Royaliste with me? They say it's the best in the entire country."

Loren's face loomed lifelike on the screen of her mind. She had already decided she couldn't bear to watch him compete for the Jumper Classic. "I—I don't know, Ted. I'll have to let you know."

"I guess I sort of shocked you coming in here like this, didn't I? I should have called."

"That's fine. I appreciate your caring enough to come. We'll talk tomorrow."

Much of Westport's population, according to their votes, still believed in Creighton Hollister's integrity—but not quite enough. He lost by a very slim margin. "Enough," he said in his early morning press conference, "so that I am encouraged to run again. And the next time, I'll have Alexandria by my side from the very beginning of the campaign."

⟡

Creighton and Lexi were in the box seats of the great civic center arena on the final night of the Royaliste Horse Show. Kassie took Ted over to introduce them.

"A fine looking young man, Kassie," Creighton said to her as he shook Ted's hand. "Is he a horse lover like you?"

"More," she confided with a grin. "If that's possible."

"Sounds quite compatible," Lexi said, her eyes shining.

"Hey there, ma'am." Ted gave a protesting arm wave. "No matchmaking, please. You'll scare Kassie plumb away from me."

Going back home to the Double-C Ranch didn't sound too bad to Kassie just now. Her insides were in knots dreading the coming event. Loren had done well in the preliminaries. Tonight would tell it all—whether or not Jolly Roger was his possession. Kassie wondered if he had the agreement in writing. Otherwise, she doubted the heartless Vaughn would give an inch, no matter how many prizes were won astride Jolly Roger.

Just across the arena from Kassie, Vaughn was sitting by the newly re-elected Mayor Bosworth. Vaughn caught her eye, and seeing Ted at her side, he gave a smug smile of satisfaction.

The events dragged out in endless succession for Kassie. Under other circumstances, she would have been taking meticulous notes on every competition, learning all she could. At one time, she had thought she might be grooming future horse show competitors at Blackburn's. Now she was unsure about her own future in Westport.

"That guy on the chestnut gelding is tight as a fiddle string," Ted was muttering beside her.

She'd been daydreaming. She looked up to see Loren ready for his jumps. Ted was right. He was more tense than she'd ever seen him at practice. She held her breath. She didn't want to let on to Ted that she even knew him. A few more minutes and the competition would all be over. She could go on living.

Jolly Roger's nostrils were flaring, his tail flipping. Kassie wanted to run out and make Loren stop. To scream at him not to care so much. To let go and let God handle everything.

Effortlessly, they cleared the first jump. Kassie saw Vaughn lean forward in his wheel chair.

The second jump was even better. Jolly Roger was sensing the glory of his performance and what it meant to Loren. Together they leaned in, turned, and gathered speed to go for the third jump, amber clouds of dust puffing out around the pounding hooves. Loren was stiffening. At the moment when he should have been slipping into the ease of the victory, he was freezing up.

Kassie wanted to look away, but her eyes were transfixed on the scene.

"For heaven's sake, man," she heard Ted mumbling again. "Loosen up and fly with it."

"He can't!" she wanted to scream. "He's let it matter too much and he can never loosen up!"

A falter on the third jump. Had Loren been in his regular form, he would have eased in and covered for it. But in his present state, it was a disaster which multiplied against itself. By the time they made the approach for the fourth jump, no one in the arena was breathing. Everyone could read the signs except Loren. On the fourth, the highest and most difficult jump, man and majestic horse went crashing together into the dust.

Kassie remembered seeing Vaughn straining at his chair, pounding the arms of the wheelchair with his fists, his hollow face drained of color. She remembered a scream, then realized it came from her own throat. Wildly, she was trying to push through the crowd and run down the aisle into the arena but Ted was holding her back with all the strength of his sinewy arms. "Kassie, you gone crazy? They don't need you down there."

Doctors were rushing onto the arena. Jolly Roger was rolling, trying desperately to stand, then falling back. Kassie could no longer control the sobs that racked her entire body. She clung to Ted and let the anguish consume her.

She made Ted drive her to the hospital, but no visitors were allowed and very little information was being given. Ted was patient with her once he understood she was no stranger to the man riding the beautiful chestnut gelding.

He held her close to him as they drove back to her apartment. "Are you in love with him?" Ted's voice came through the hazy cloud. His tenderness and caring were clear in his tone.

She could only nod.

"Was it all over?"

"Yes." Her fist was pressed hard against her mouth.

He parked in front of Mom Tinsley's house, looming large and white in the moonlight. Helping her out, he said, "I saw that pretty garden out back. Let's take a little walk."

She followed by his side.

"Look, Kassie," he said. "I know this must have been more of a devastating evening for you than I could ever imagine, but I have to leave in two days. My talking time's short. Come back with me, Kassie. Come home where you belong. You've given this place a fair try. You've done your best."

Honeysuckle fragrances wafted about them on soft waves. Ted's understanding nature amazed her. He was right. She *had* done her best. But now Loren didn't want her, nor did Glorene. What good would it do to stay?

"I'm not asking you to marry me now. You're a wonderful person, and I've loved you for a long time. I'm willing to wait a while longer, till you warm up to the idea. I believe we can have a wonderful marriage. One that will grow strong. I can give you everything you've ever wanted, plus your own home ranch. Just come back for a time, then decide. That fair?"

His words poured over her wounds like soothing ointment. She looked up at his face in the moonlight. His angular face with the high cheekbones was not handsome, but she saw a simple strength there. Ted, she knew, shared her faith. She could do a lot worse than spend the rest of her life with this gentle rancher.

She nodded. "That's fair. I'll be packed and ready to leave on Monday morning. But you'll have to give me time to heal. Much has happened to me here."

He stepped toward her and put his arm loosely about her shoulder. "I'm a patient man, Kassie."

She turned to bury her face in his chest. Would there ever be a time when she could give herself to Ted and not wish he were Loren?

A call to the hospital the next morning revealed that Loren had been released after an overnight stay with a few broken ribs and a broken wrist. *A miracle he wasn't hurt worse,* Kassie thought.

She decided she should tell Glorene in person that she was going home. But when she got there, Leomia said Glorene was gone. "She's out of town. Didn't say where. Just said she had to get away. After the election loss and all."

Kassie nodded, smothered in Leomia's hug. She explained her decision to go back to Wyoming and told her she'd come to say good-bye.

"Going back with Mr. Winters, I suspect?"

"For a while, at least. Until I get my directions straight."

"You could do that here. Don't forget your grandfather's request."

"I haven't forgotten, but I've tried and failed here. Wyoming will always be home."

"And what about the opportunities at Blackburn's? You weren't a failure there. And your work with Lexi? That wasn't a failure. There are other Lexis you know. And other Mindys too for that matter."

Kassie shook her head. "Please, Leomia, don't confuse me. I have some heavy decisions to make."

"Sure you do. So make your decisions by looking at all the angles, not just Glorene and Loren."

"I've made the first decision—I'm packing and leaving Monday. I may return some day. Who knows?"

Leomia took her hand. "No one can blame you. I love you and wish you every happiness. And don't be too hard on Glorene. The last chapter on her hasn't been written yet."

❧

Kassie planned to say good-by to Regalia alone. Even with the knowledge that she would soon see Onrushing Charger again, parting from her new companion would be hard.

She now had her own keys to the stables and decided at the last minute to walk over. The June evening was mellow and warm, and the two-mile walk, she knew, would be good for her.

As she let herself in and strolled past the glassed-in office, she admired the neat interior. She had succeeded in bringing the place back to life. She hoped the one who followed in her steps would take as good care of the office. Between Loren, Creighton, and Harlis, surely they would teach the new replacement the ropes. However, Kassie had initiated a few things that no one knew about.

Perhaps, she should write them down before she left. But first, Regalia!

"Regalia! Hi there, girl. What's going on?"

A soft nicker sounded in response. She opened the door to the stall. This horse grew more exquisite with each passing day. Her head was high and lofty, her neck grandly arched. Her bright eyes were never clouded with rebellion. Jolly Roger's stall was empty. He was still at the vet's. Harlis had told her they were hoping the horse's front leg would heal correctly. No one knew for sure just yet.

"Hey, girl. I've come to say thank you and good-bye." Kassie stroked the muscular shoulders. "You've been so good to me and I love you for it. How about one last ride? Okay?"

Crying time is over, she scolded herself as she dabbed at her eyes with her sleeve. The noises of lifting the saddle from the frame and heaving it over Regalia's back prevented her from hearing the side door open and close.

Loren didn't want to frighten her, but he let himself watch for a few moments as her slender Levi-clad form deftly geared her horse to ride. When she turned to lead Regalia from the stall, he could see her tear-stained face shining in the dim light.

"Kassie?" Softly, so as not to startle her, he stepped toward her.

Something deep inside her knew immediately who the shadowy figure was. "Loren." She gripped the reins more tightly in her hand. "How's the wrist?"

He held up the arm, the white cast gleaming. "Doing pretty well. Healing fast." He touched his side. "The ribs hurt, though."

"It was a rough fall. Worst I've ever seen." She wished he hadn't come. Leaving would be even more difficult now.

"Glorene's in Florida."

"Is she?"

"She said to tell you she went to see Ben."

Kassie leaned her head into the arch of Regalia's warm velvet neck. "Well, well. What do you know?"

"She was pretty washed out about the election loss and all."

She nodded.

"And I was a little washed out myself—but not about the election."

"How's Jolly Roger?"

"The final reports aren't in. He'll never jump again, we know that much. Ironic." He leaned his torso against the arena railing. "Now that we're both losers, Dad has no interest in either me or Jolly Roger. The horse is mine now free and clear."

Regalia snorted and stamped her foot, impatient for the exercise she'd been promised.

"I should have listened to you about Sean. He was worse than a spider."

"I should have listened to you too, Kassie. About a lot of things. Because of my bitterness toward Dad and my desire to get Jolly Roger, I lost it all. I wanted to show Dad I was as good as Roger. I had the head to win, didn't I? But not the heart."

"Loren..." she protested. For him to punish himself was useless.

"Be honest."

"Not the heart," she agreed.

"Roger had the heart, right?"

She nodded again.

"And even good old Creighton. He really had a heart to win, didn't he? Even if it meant losing. See how well I'm learning?" He took the reins from her hand and led Regalia into the arena, tied her there, and came back to stand before Kassie.

"And little Kassie. Precious Kassie has a heart to win for her Lord even if it means losing."

He lifted her chin to look full at her face. "I'm beginning to understand now. Actually I knew at Mindy's funeral. I never heard anyone speak of eternity like Mindy's mother did. At that moment, I knew I wanted to give my life to the Lord. But still there was that stubborn streak, that last holdout. I lay in the hospital the other night feeling sorry for myself because of all that had happened to me. I was totally humiliated by the fall. Then I remembered what you'd said about God's grace. Everything I've touched has backfired. I lost everything, and I thought I'd lost you. So I turned it all over to Him."

He wrapped her snugly in his arms and held her tightly. Tears burned hot in her eyes.

"I know the sweetness of His forgiveness. And the depth of His peace. When I prayed and invited Him to take over, that tormenting hatred for Dad just melted away." He pulled her still tighter. "Can you ever forgive me for venting my anger on you? It was Sean who loosened the cinch, wasn't it?"

"On orders from your father."

"If I had known that night, I would have torn him apart. In front of everyone."

"Good thing you didn't know. It would have been a waste of time. He'll be torn apart soon enough."

"I was such a fool. Can you let me start all over again? Could *we* start all over again?"

Not waiting for her answer, he released her to reach into his jacket pocket. "I was determined not to come to you without this." He handed her a paper which rustled in her trembling hands.

"A contract? To buy the stables? How did you...?"

"Creighton's agreed to sell, and he's given us a fantastic deal."

"Us?"

"Of course, us. He believes you and I can make it a great success. And so do I. The Marcellus Stables, owned and operated by Mr. and Mrs. Loren Marcellus."

Kassie could scarcely believe what she was hearing. "But what about school? Your exams?"

"I'm dropping Roger's dreams. I'm a business major and a horse lover. I'd make a lousy lawyer. Isn't that what you tried to tell me?"

She smiled. "I did."

"Leomia said you were leaving to go back to Wyoming with that rancher guy. Am I too late, Kassie? Did I let things go too far?"

Ted had said he was a patient man. Surely the Lord would send the perfect girl for him. One who would love him as he deserved to be loved—as Kassie never could.

Kassie gazed up at Loren's translucent blue eyes. They were clear now. She saw the relaxed smile, the one she'd glimpsed the day of the trail ride. The one that had lit the light inside of her. So Grandpa Carver had been right after all. She *had* been destined to come to Virginia.

A joy swept over her as she responded to his embrace with the love so long repressed. She reached up and traced one deep dimple with her fingertip. "Don't you know, my precious Loren," she said as she placed her own heartfelt kisses on his face and lips, "it's never too late—for someone who has a *real* heart to win!"

A Letter To Our Readers

Dear Reader:

In order that we might better contribute to your reading enjoyment, we would appreciate your taking a few minutes to respond to the following questions. When completed, please return to the following:

Rebecca Germany, Editor
Heartsong Presents
P.O. Box 719
Uhrichsville, Ohio 44683

1. Did you enjoy reading *The Winning Heart*?
   ❏ Very much. I would like to see more books
      by this author!
   ❏ Moderately
      I would have enjoyed it more if _____

   _____

2. Are you a member of *Heartsong Presents*? Yes   No
   If no, where did you purchase this book? _____

   _____

3. What influenced your decision to purchase this
   book? (Check those that apply.)

   ❏ Cover   ❏ Back cover copy

   ❏ Title   ❏ Friends

   ❏ Publicity   ❏ Other _____

4. On a scale from 1 (poor) to 10 (superior), please rate the following elements.

    ___Heroine   ___Plot

    ___Hero   ___Inspirational theme

    ___Setting   ___Secondary characters

5. What settings would you like to see covered in *Heartsong Presents* books?

_____

_____

6. What are some inspirational themes you would like to see treated in future books?_____

_____

_____

7. Would you be interested in reading other *Heartsong Presents* titles?   ❑ Yes   ❑ No

8. Please check your age range:
❑ Under 18   ❑ 18-24   ❑ 25-34
❑ 35-45   ❑ 46-55   ❑ Over 55

9. How many hours per week do you read? _____

Name _____

Occupation _____

Address _____

City _____ State _____ Zip _____

Brenda Bancroft

___*Indy Girl*—After the tragic deaths of her famous brother and father, Amanda Jane Stacy is left to fulfill the family legacy and race in the Indy 500. Then Dan Barenfanger enters her life. Not only is this dashingly handsome man a great asset to her racing team, but he's also made an impression on her heart as well. HP22 $2.95

___*A Love Meant To Be*—When Bill Sterling, Alana Charles's former fiancé reenters her life after a two-year, unexplained absence, strange things begin to happen to her. Bill is a likely suspect, but he maintains that he is a changed man. Time is not on Alana's side. . .and neither is the power to believe. HP30 $2.95

___*When Comes the Dawn*—When Amity Sheffield's married half-sister arranges for Amity to marry their dour cousin, Amity is left with no choice. She might never again see Jeb Dennison, a handsome Rebel whose lips are mute but whose eyes speak only of love, but she is determined to be faithful to him. HP35 $2.95

___*A Real and Precious Thing*—Which man does God want for Loralie Morgan—Jonathan McGuire or Denis St. John? With Jonathan, she feels contented and comfortable, as though they have known each other forever. She and Denis don't even trust each other yet. . .deep down Loralie wonders, is this the real thing? HP62 $2.95

*Watch for *There's Always Tomorrow* (HP122) coming soon from Heartsong Presents.

Send to: Heartsong Presents Reader's Service
P.O. Box 719
Uhrichsville, Ohio 44683

Please send me the items checked above. I am enclosing
$_____(please add $1.00 to cover postage and handling
per order. OH add 6.25% tax. NJ add 6% tax.).
Send check or money order, no cash or C.O.D.s, please.
   To place a credit card order, call 1-800-847-8270.

NAME _____

ADDRESS _____

CITY/STATE _____ ZIP _____

....Hearts ♥ ng ....

Any 12 *Heartsong Presents* titles for only $26.95 *

CONTEMPORARY ROMANCE IS CHEAPER BY THE DOZEN!

Buy any assortment of twelve *Heartsong Presents* titles and save 25% off of the already discounted price of $2.95 each!

*plus $1.00 shipping and handling per order and sales tax where applicable.

HEARTSONG PRESENTS TITLES AVAILABLE NOW:

__HP 3 RESTORE THE JOY, *Sara Mitchell*
__HP 5 THIS TREMBLING CUP, *Marlene Chase*
__HP 6 THE OTHER SIDE OF SILENCE, *Marlene Chase*
__HP 9 HEARTSTRINGS, *Irene B. Brand*
__HP 10 SONG OF LAUGHTER, *Lauraine Snelling*
__HP 13 PASSAGE OF THE HEART, *Kjersti Hoff Baez*
__HP 14 A MATTER OF CHOICE, *Susannah Hayden*
__HP 21 GENTLE PERSUASION, *Veda Boyd Jones*
__HP 22 INDY GIRL, *Brenda Bancroft*
__HP 25 REBAR, *Mary Carpenter Reid*
__HP 26 MOUNTAIN HOUSE, *Mary Louise Colln*
__HP 29 FROM THE HEART, *Sara Mitchell*
__HP 30 A LOVE MEANT TO BE, *Brenda Bancroft*
__HP 33 SWEET SHELTER, *VeraLee Wiggins*
__HP 34 UNDER A TEXAS SKY, *Veda Boyd Jones*
__HP 37 DRUMS OF SHELOMOH, *Yvonne Lehman*
__HP 38 A PLACE TO CALL HOME, *Eileen M. Berger*
__HP 41 FIELDS OF SWEET CONTENT, *Norma Jean Lutz*
__HP 42 SEARCH FOR TOMORROW, *Mary Hawkins*
__HP 45 DESIGN FOR LOVE, *Janet Gortsema*
__HP 46 THE GOVERNOR'S DAUGHTER, *Veda Boyd Jones*
__HP 49 YESTERDAY'S TOMORROWS, *Linda Herring*
__HP 50 DANCE IN THE DISTANCE, *Kjersti Hoff Baez*
__HP 53 MIDNIGHT MUSIC, *Janelle Burnham*
__HP 54 HOME TO HER HEART, *Lena Nelson Dooley*
__HP 57 LOVE'S SILKEN MELODY, *Norma Jean Lutz*
__HP 58 FREE TO LOVE, *Doris English*
__HP 61 PICTURE PERFECT, *Susan Kirby*
__HP 62 A REAL AND PRECIOUS THING, *Brenda Bancroft*
__HP 65 ANGEL FACE, *Frances Carfi Matranga*
__HP 66 AUTUMN LOVE, *Ann Bell*
__HP 69 BETWEEN LOVE AND LOYALTY, *Susannah Hayden*
__HP 70 A NEW SONG, *Kathleen Yapp*

(If ordering from this page, please remember to include it with the order form.)

.... Presents ....

__HP 73 MIDSUMMER'S DREAM, *Rena Eastman*
__HP 74 SANTANONI SUNRISE, *Hope Irvin Marston and Claire M. Coughlin*
__HP 77 THE ROAD BEFORE ME, *Susannah Hayden*
__HP 78 A SIGN OF LOVE, *Veda Boyd Jones*
__HP 81 BETTER THAN FRIENDS, *Sally Laity*
__HP 82 SOUTHERN GENTLEMEN, *Yvonne Lehman*
__HP 85 LAMP IN DARKNESS, *Connie Loraine*
__HP 86 POCKETFUL OF LOVE, *Loree Lough*
__HP 89 CONTAGIOUS LOVE, *Ann Bell*
__HP 90 CATER TO A WHIM, *Norma Jean Lutz*
__HP 93 IDITAROD DREAM, *Janelle Jamison*
__HP 94 TO BE STRONG, *Carolyn R. Scheidies*
__HP 97 A MATCH MADE IN HEAVEN, *Kathleen Yapp*
__HP 98 BEAUTY FOR ASHES, *Becky Melby and Cathy Wienke*
__HP101 DAMAGED DREAMS, *Mary Hawkins*
__HP102 IF GIVEN A CHOICE, *Tracie J. Peterson*
__HP105 CIRCLE OF LOVE, *Alma Blair*
__HP106 RAGDOLL, *Kelly R. Stevens*
__HP109 INSPIRED LOVE, *Ann Bell*
__HP110 CALLIE'S MOUNTAIN, *Veda Boyd Jones*
__HP113 BETWEEN THE MEMORY AND THE MOMENT, *Susannah Hayden*
__HP114 THE QUIET HEART, *Rae Simons*
__HP117 FARTHER ALONG THE ROAD, *Susannah Hayden*
__HP118 FLICKERING FLAMES, *Connie Loraine*
__HP121 THE WINNING HEART, *Norma Jean Lutz*
__HP122 THERE'S ALWAYS TOMORROW, *Brenda Bancroft*

Great Inspirational Romance at a Great Price!

Heartsong Presents books are inspirational romances in contemporary and historical settings, designed to give you an enjoyable, spirit-lifting reading experience.   You can choose from 124 wonderfully written titles from some of today's best authors like Colleen L. Reece, Brenda Bancroft, Janelle Jamison, and many others.

When ordering quantities less than twelve, above titles are $2.95 each.